BREAKFAST AT BABS'

SIMON PETERS

ACKNOWLEDGEMENTS

To my Wife Carol and our Children who have always supported me, and have put up with the chaotic lifestyle of a serviceman.

That same lifestyle gave me the motivation to write this book, in which I try to convey as true a feeling of 'just getting on with the job' as is possible.

I would also like to dedicate this book to all those who have served their country often without hesitation or question, and also the general public, friends and families who have supported those men and women who choose to serve whatever their true feelings or beliefs. It is for our feelings and beliefs that they continue to lay down their lives.

Finally I would like to thank Babs and Carol who were always there, remembered every name, every girlfriend or Wife, and never forgot an outstanding breakfast chit at the end of the month!

Prologue

They had been watching the same sun bleached wooden door for 3 days now, its varnish browned, and peeling in long crackled strips. 2 days ago a small white bus had arrived, its paint battered by years of sun and sharp windblown sand, its brakes squealing like a trapped animal as it slowed and came to a halt outside the door old door.

They were expecting it, and had been waiting for it. They watched quietly and carefully as a tall well dressed man wearing smart trousers, although a little tight and a fawn chequered shirt climbed out of the passenger door. He looked a little under 40; his dark hair was long, dry and unkempt, with a few wisps of grey. A pair of gold rimmed Ray Ban Aviators shielded his eyes from the bright afternoon sun.

A white Mercedes saloon passed the bus, and drew up a little way ahead, another could just be seen behind the bus, a little further down the road. Both were covered in a thick coat of dirt and dust, they rested on their suspension as if they had been driven from across the other side of the world. On further examination the watcher noticed that all the tyres on the vehicles looked abnormally low. Maybe to aid grip on the loose and inhospitable terrain that surrounded the small town on every side, maybe that had travelled from much further afield.

One occupant emerged from each of the Mercedes', from the front car a women in a dull and very dusty black burke her head covered in an equally dirty black Chador, appeared by the passenger door. She walked cautiously around to stand in front of the cars bonnet, the white paint hidden by layers of dust and dirt. They watched her as she continuously inspected her surroundings, she scanned up and down the dust and rubble road, and one by one examined the mostly derelict two story buildings that flanked the small kerbs in both directions.

Obviously satisfied that all was clear, she looked back towards the tall man by the minibus, and nodded. He in turn looked down the street at a large stocky man, wearing a dark jacket, his head protected from the sun in a red and white chequered shemagh head scarf. Protruding from his thick beard was a dark coloured cigarette, he had been scanning down the road in the opposite direction, looking back he too now nodded.

The tall man approached the wooden door, drawing a large iron key from his pocket, he unlocked the door, and pushed it open, with only dry sand for lubrication the iron hinge screamed with the binding of the metal against metal. He turned and stood for a moment with his back to the door and then with an urgent hand ushered to the minibus's other as yet unseen occupants.

A flash of white was seen as 2 children rushed forward and in through the door, their shoes could be heard tapping as they raced across the wooden floor, the sound echoing from open door.

The boots popped open on both of the saloons and the man and the women grabbed several bags from their own cars, shuttling them to the front door where the tall man hauled them into the front entrance.

They counted 8 small gym bags, all identical in colour, Navy Blue, with red piping, at first the watcher assumed that they containing the children's belongings, but 8? Then from each car a further two bags appeared, they were black, large and heavy gauge hold-alls. They were obviously heavy as they watched the women struggle to haul hers one at a time from the deep boot of the car, once safely on the floor, she half lifted and half dragged them one by one up to the door step, where they too were then hauled inside.

The women and the large man disappeared inside, leaving only the tall man on the step to the house. He took one last look up and down the street, and with a quick waving of the back of his hand the minibus driver pulled away, followed by the two escorts in a cloud of dust and black exhaust fumes.

As the sound of the vehicles faded the door was closed slowly, screeching in pain as it did so, and even from across the street the watchers heard the heavy bolt clank as it was locked.

It had now been 2 days since they had arrived, no one else had arrived and no one had left, the door had not opened not even to allow someone to go to the local market.

The observation post was located on the opposite side of the small deserted street. From their covert vantage point in the upper floor of the old and for the most part dilapidated building they could see directly in through the second floor windows above the old cracking door.

The small window that the telescope was pointing through was one of the few with some glass left in it. Cut into it, and above a rusting sink, was an old metal ventilator which very rarely span in the hot still air. When it did spin the bearings screeched once every turn, making the occupants wince from the noise. It seemed so loud in the relative silence it would surely give their position away.

On the other side of the street and above the old door the two large windows of the old apartment were dusty, and streaked with lines of dirt left by the heavy rains that had fallen some months before.

The second and largest window had a large crack in the bottom corner of its single pane of glass, hanging either side was a heavy pair of ancient, and faded curtains, which looked more like an old red Persian rug that had been torn in two. Now the drapes had a new life as they framed a stage, its players not knowing they had an observant audience.

Fortunately for the watchers the curtains were left open during the long hot days, exposing the cracked window, probably to try to catch the wisp of a draft in the dry airless heat.

Through this window a disturbing show was about to be performed. There was more movement now, they watching as two children sat at a long blue and faded vinyl covered table, which had been conveniently placed by the window.

They had decided the eldest, a boy, was around 12 to 14 years old, and the younger girl about 8. The team had taken dozens of digital photos of them both, and after careful examination decided that they were almost certainly brother and sister.

They were receiving another lesson, on what no one was sure yet. The tall man at the door seemed to have a new role as a teacher, the teacher always appeared smartly dressed, and always in a chequered shirt, with his Ray Bans in his shirt pocket.

Today his shirt was blue and white, just as he had appeared in the grainy photograph that they had been given during their brief by a nervous local operative 2 weeks before, the briefing had been exactly that, brief.

They were not given the normal detailed analysis and mission directive, but told only when and where to look, a picture of the main target and to make a snatch as soon as they had anything incriminating, and felt able to do so.

The only part of the orders that were specific were that once they had made contact, not to lose sight of the principle target. More agents and resources were coming but not immediately and they were on their own with no support for the time being everyone was determined not to fuck up.

The man they had nick named 'the teacher' had spent most of the afternoon pacing up and down the room, only occasionally as he passed the window was he in line of sight of the observers.

Now he was stood at the end of the table in front of the children. In his hands he held out a green faded canvas bag. He spoke first to the girl, her back to the observers they could see only the top of her head and her turquoise head scarf, glittering with sequins. He motioned and she stood up from behind the table and approached her teacher.

They watched as he helped her put the canvas bag over her out held arms, even from this view point they could tell it was heavy as the girl struggled to pull the straps over her small shoulders. She turned around and leant forward as the teacher helped her adjust the load.

Under the careful direction of the teacher the girl turned slowly and carefully, walking around the room and out of sight for a few seconds. When she reappeared she faced her teacher and smiled broadly, as if she had received a gift. Now facing the window the watcher refocused the telescope and all became clear, the green canvas pockets were bulging with brown lumps that were clearly not school books. Wires ran from the top of each of the 5 pockets across the young girl's chest to her small hand wrapped tightly around the small dark cylinder that was quite obviously the firing device. She smiled down at her older brother her smile beaming with pride.

The teacher motioned with his hand for her to walk around once again. She walked in and out of view, it was obvious that the bomb was very heavy on her delicate frame. She stopped occasionally to adjust the weight on her shoulders, then walked out of sight again. A few minutes later she reappeared, the teacher helped her remove the device and the girl sat back down in her original seat.

The watchers looked at each other in disbelief, not able to even find the words to speak. Now it was the boys turn, they watched as the boy went through the same routine, his equipment a little bulkier than the girls, he too strutted proudly around the room, stopping in front of the table he stood like a stallion before his sister proud and virtuous.

The boy turned again with his back to the window, now once again facing his teacher. The teacher seemed to look past the boy, over his shoulder and out through the window, he looked wildly self-possessed as he smiled broadly.

As dusk approached the activity in the flat became more hectic than on previous nights, and all the occupants seemed to be in an anxious state. The children were sat opposite each other at the table; they had been brought food by the female. They had seen her moving around the house as she did the chores, and fed everyone their meals. Inside she no longer wore a Burke but normally something bright. On this occasion she wore a red velvet track suit top, with silver tram lines on the sleeves, and on her head a red and silver scarf, the silver sequins flashing in the artificial light.

The children sat with a large plate of rice and some meat, they ate with metal forks and spoons, and continued to read undisturbed. Often pointing at pages and discussing parts of the text they were so absorbed in. Meanwhile the man with the beard and the women were busy around them, moving from room to room moving bags and collecting belongings. The teacher had stayed in the main room, pacing back and forward, and in and out of view, he had been busy making and receiving calls on at least 3 different mobile phones.

One of the watchers looked around, the soft moonlight reflecting off of her coffee skin, her dark hair short and a little matted with the dust. She spoke with a soft American accent, in the back ground of her voice was a slight hint of her Persian roots. 'Hey Toni, they're on the move. It's now or never, get the gear away in the grab bags and wake the others........quickly.'

Breakfast at Babs'

The tall dark man was stood back from the window operating the digital camera and the telescope, and watching from a small LCD screen under a black cloth. Toni Marino had only transferred last year from the NYPD, this was his first real field assignment with the CIA, he had spent most of the last year on training courses, cultural familiarisation and learning Arabic, he had spent the last two months as a field and technical data analyst in Baghdad, there to learn the ropes for a year or more, or that was the plan.

It had come as a complete surprise when he was suddenly assigned to a penetration team, he was told it was because of his past experience on a SWAT team, and so he had some of the skills required. He had had plenty of time in the last few weeks and especially the last few days to wonder if it was really a good idea as he had struggled to learn on the job, he had to admit that even the CIA must be seriously short of experienced people, or just had too much work on now!

Exhilarated, and shit scared all at the same time, he was keen to impress his somewhat bossy and arrogant team leader, 'Okay, sure ma'am'.

They had been through the plan several times before, and had already walked the route several times. When they had arrived the door out into the corridor was only just hanging on by the top hinge, the bottom hinge had rusted away. Toni armed with a multi tool had removed one from another door and replaced it, then used gun oil to stop it squeaking, this had won him a few points, but no direct praise.

In the dark the four agents moved quietly back through the door and carefully down the concrete and stone stairs to one of the bottom flats. They moved in two groups, the woman and Toni moved into the ground floor apartment and waited by a large window which like most of the others had long since lost its glass. This was the only place where they could clearly see the old wooden door that accessed the terrorist's upstairs apartment, now directly across the street. The only obstacle between them and the other side of the street was an old burnt out taxi, which had ended its career a few meters from their concealed position. Like Taxi's all over the region it was a Mercedes the only clue to its former colour a faded blue door laying on its side some distance away.

The second team moved down the corridor to what would have been the front door, which was now a large hole barricaded up to waist height with assorted junk, including an old TV with the screen smashed, half a rusty bike and various pieces of charred clothes, carpet and wood. From here they could only just see the edge of the terrorist's exit point, but their job was to cut off any escape attempt up the road.

Their earpieces crackled with the sound of a female voice, 'OK upstairs lights have gone out, expect all targets on the move'.

The front door slowly screeched open and after a brief moment the bearded male and then the female, stepped cautiously out onto the street, each observing in a different direction, carefully checking both up and down the street. The female was once again dressed in a black burke and glanced briefly up at the very room the agents had been observing from. She then turned her head and nodded at her partner, he reached now under his clothes and pulled out a lighter from his robe. There was a flash of light as he lit up a cigarette.

'Hold positions, there's the signal' Jo's voice once again crackled over the ear piece.

From further down the street an engine could be heard, shortly followed by some lights, the same small white battered minibus that had first delivered the teacher and two children two days ago came into view. The women held her left arm up to her head to shield her eye's before the driver switched the headlights off as he slowed down and pulled up outside the door.

'OK we can do this, no one moves until they're in the open'.

Breakfast at Babs'

Timing was critical, too soon and all you get is the henchmen, too late and you lose them into the night.

The door opened a little wider, and from Toni's position it was hard to see the two smaller figures as they came through the door, she could just make out the tops of the heads through the minibus windows. Then the man in the chequered shirt came into view.

In the earpiece the woman's voice whispered her orders, 'OK guys this is it three....two....one....go'

Toni followed close behind Jo as she broke from the cover of their hideout, and ran directly toward the mini bus.

In her right hand her automatic pistol levelled and her left arm raised hand extended screaming 'STOP....STOP, STOP NOW'. She shouted whilst pointing at the driver, 'YOU STOP THE FUCKIN BUS'.

It all happened so quickly as these things always did: pick the right target or he'll pick you.

Jo ran forward to the front of the mini bus, a glance at the driver showed that he was terrified, but not an immediate threat. She canted her gun and pointed it directly at him, she was looking up the street for the other women.

To her right Toni now came around the burnt out taxi to cover the terrorist with the cigarette, he was twisting now, his AK47 coming up on aim. Jo, his target was now clearly lit up by the minibus side lights.

Toni already had his target he fired two shots in quick succession which found their target. He watched as the wounded man fell against the wall he dropped his gun on its butt, a single shot rang out from the AK47, a lone green tracer bullet arced up into the night sky. The bearded man staggered down the wall a little way and fell from the curb, rolling behind the bus. Toni looked for the wounds but the red side lights of the bus hid any blood escaping from his chest, making him look to the casual observer as if he had fallen asleep on the pavement smoking his black cigarette.

The agent ran forward to confirm his kill, taking up a new position behind the bus next to the dead terrorist. From where he knelt he was able to cover the back of the bus and the apartment door, he was aware that inside the bus were two very frightened children.

To the left the other pair had swung out across the street to cover the female terrorist, shouting at her to put her gun down. She just stared at them as they ran towards her, her weapon fired from the hip initially, automatic fire mixed with the occasional green tracer rained down in their direction. Her aim improved as the weapon was brought up into the shoulder, but luckily for the guys still using automatic fire, and so wasting her ammunition with generally inaccurate fire. She was missing but it still had the desired effect: and they both dove for cover, and this gave her just enough time to dive into a doorway, seeking cover to reload with a fresh magazine.

The driver had frozen, the school teacher was shouting at him from the back of the minibus.

Then Jo shouted again, 'EVERYONE OUT OF THE BUS...NOW!' she didn't think to use Arabic, and didn't give a fuck if they could understand English or not. Indicating with her gun should have made her orders obvious enough to anyone; anyone at least who did not want a bullet in the head. The driver's door slowly began to open. From the rear the teacher in the chequered shirt was shouting at the driver, in an obvious attempt to persuade him to drive on. In a desperate panic he threw himself forward, barging past the two children throwing them down hard against the upholstery. The driver froze, a firm hand was gripping his shoulder, his temple registering the cold hard metal of a pistol, she heard 'Yella Yella', as he screamed at the driver in Arabic.

Confused Jo switched her aim to the man in the chequered shirt, it was hard to pick him out clearly in dim interior, and she knew there was at least one child in the seat somewhere between them. She hesitated, the van revved and lurched forward, the man in the chequered shirt was staring coolly at her through the windscreen.

The two agents down the street wondered why no more gun fire had come their way. Looking almost simultaneously ahead of them they could see Jo silhouetted by the front lights of the minibus. Her dark hair in a bun she was standing shouting in Arabic at the vehicle. They watched as the minibus lights brightened, and as the bus turned away from the curb and in their direction. Just before the lights blinded them they saw the women in her black robes taking careful aim with her AK47. The 2 agents jumped up together shouting and raising their pistols, everywhere weapons sang out, both women fell at the same time.

They heard a metallic clunk as the minibus side door rolled back and slammed shut by the sudden forward momentum. They watched Jo spin from the bullet in her shoulder and directly into the front of the bus as it slammed her down, but it was the driver's front wheel slamming over her wounded body that turned a shoulder wound into a fatality.

On the floor the woman in black was clearly wounded, but managed to take aim at Toni laying behind the minibus now suddenly lit up by the tail lights of the escaping vehicle.

Toni was now a sitting duck his only cover the dead body of the cigarette smoking corpse. He raised his gun and fired a couple of rounds in return, but the weight of fire from the automatic assault rifle was too much. Toni knew if he stayed the bullets would find him, but he had frozen, unable to move. He took a breath, and somehow found the courage to persuade his muscles they had a job to do. At that moment he heard his name 'Toni…Toni move now, we got you' and then the sound of rounds being fired to cover him, he made a sudden dash for the cover of the doorway.

The other 2 agents had put the fire down just in time, they could no longer see past the bus rapidly approaching them, its bright head lights now blinding them. They both now knelt, shooting at the driver as he approached, aware that there were 2 frightened children somewhere inside; the driver swerved the bus erratically as he somehow managed to survive the ambush.

He careered past them both; his bolt for freedom was however short lived. The popping sound 10 meters down the road signalled that his tyres had hit the spiked caltrops chain. Thrown by the cut off team as they had initially dashed across the road. The spikes bit into all 4 tyres deflating them quickly, slowing the minibus and making it heavy, and sluggish. They heard the engine roar as the driver pushed down hard on the accelerator pedal trying to keep up the speed. Sparks were now shooting from the rear of the vehicle as a tyre was ripped from the rim, the vehicle was rapidly slowing.

Desperately the driver dropped through the gears to try to keep up some momentum. He turned hard to the left, knowing this was the way back onto the main market street and now his only chance of escape. Struggling to manoeuvre the minibus the turn was too tight and the minibus leant heavily over, it glanced off of the large curb stone, and scraped down a dark disused lamppost, the metal on metal threw out a festival of sparks.

Back at the apartment the gun fight ensued, Toni was now relatively safe, but outgunned, he was backed into the doorway and reloading his pistol. The 2 agents knew that Toni was not going to fight his way out alone, and in desperate need of help, but someone should go after the minibus, that was where the high value target was.

Ignoring the screeching minibus they both began to lay some fire down to give their colleague time. It was obvious to everyone that the woman was a true fanatic and going to fight to the death. Toni was reloaded and the battle ensued. Toni glanced from his cover and saw in the failing light a glimpse of black shoulder and quickly shot twice, he missed and concrete splinters sheared off the wall.

In return a hail of Automatic fire showered his doorframe, concrete and wood was splintering in all directions, the sheer noise making Toni cower again. Then the automatic fire ceased, with his heart pounding Toni waited, she must be reloading, shit this is my chance.

Toni emerged from his doorway, his pistol up ready, he watched as she turned and raised her AK47, aiming down the street at the two agents. Just as he had pulled the first pressure on his trigger he noticed that her magazine was missing. She had run out of ammunition, instead of giving up or running and believing her task now complete she was aiming to die. Toni sprang forward shouting at the other 2 agents, 'NO, don't shoot'. He was too late as 8 shots rang out and ensured her place next to her cigarette smoking husband, and her journey to her God as a Martyr.

As Toni stepped forward to check the body, he looked down the road and called to the other two, pointing down the road 'I'm Okay, you fella's get after the bus'

Toni ran over to see if Jo was still alive, he placed his fingers on her neck feeling for the carotid pulse, he was not surprised to feel nothing there.

He then began to search the other bodies, starting with the male body that he had been hiding behind. 100 metres down the street the 2 other agents were running toward the mini bus, now laying on its side with the tail lights still on.

The side door was now where the roof should have been, trying to escape out of it was the man in the chequered shirt. The first agent pulled him down and cuffed him with plastic cable ties, and then they helped out the 2 children who were both screaming, and in tears, both still wearing head scarfs. Still sat in his seat the driver was quite obviously dead, half his head splattered across the driver's window.

They loosely cuffed the 2 children together by one hand and began to march them back around the corner to meet up with Toni, and hopefully Jo. As they turned the corner they could see Toni in the dim yellow lamp light leaning over the women in black, pulling her over to check her. The street light up with a flash and large explosion resonated through the street, the explosion channelled by the buildings pushed a huge pressure wave towards them. The lamppost in front of them collapsed, and they were all thrown back, and slammed to the ground. Numbed and struggling to their feet leaving their charges they ran back towards the apartment, everywhere ahead was burning. The side of the apartment was missing, rubble strew across the road. Lying where the female terrorist should have been was Toni's body, and what was left of his torso was on fire.

Driving away in the far distance was a white Mercedes car. Behind them the man in the chequered shirt began to laugh, something was wrong, he now appeared a lot older than he had done in the flat. Smiling at them from the handcuffs were 2 un-familiar small boys of about 10 years old.

Chapter 1
Cold Wet Nights

It had already been a long year of training and exercises, the year had started during a particularly cold Norwegian winter with nearly 3 months of arctic training.

It was a traditional training ground for the Royal Marines who had first landed at Narvik to fight the Germans in 1940, and the Corps had been back year after year since the 1970's. The training areas were 200 miles inside the Arctic Circle, steep jagged Mountains and deep unforgiving Fjords. The harsh environment taught a soldier to look after himself and his kit, you had to first survive the cold, before you could fight, it didn't suit everyone but it was a unique and extremely demanding training ground. The saying went if you could survive here you could survive anywhere, which was not too far from the truth.

Driving an open boat such as the 8 metre fibre glass Rigid Raiding Craft at 30 knots through the unforgiving Norwegian Fjords was gruelling, but exhilarating. With the wind chill, the temperature would often drop to –

30°C, icicles would form quickly on any exposed metal, on masts, instruments and even the coxswains noses and moustaches grown especially for the season. The troops of Marines that they dashed around the Fjords had to stay as dry as possible, and frostbite free so they were fit to fight when they were landed, almost exclusively at night. Navigation was conducted with a compass and stop watch, GPS batteries never lasting more than a few minutes in the sub zero temperatures. On arriving at their drop off points the coxswains often had to smash through ice to get to the rocky and slippery beaches, to deliver their load of fellow Commandoes.

The last few days had been spent in Narvik on RnR, spending most of what had been saved on expensive frothy beer that only came in halves, most of which was foam.

On return to the UK spring was in the air and there followed a couple of weeks leave, a brief period catching up on family and friends .Then a long anticipated trip across the Atlantic, a 2 month exercise in America, working and training alongside the US Marines in South Carolina on the East coast. Once teh exercises were complete everyone had made the most of the R & R package, some of the guys had even hitchhiked all the way down to Florida taking advantage of a typical American enthusiasm and friendliness; generous and thankful of their British cousins, who had stood shoulder to shoulder with their young men in Afghanistan and Iraq.

It was now September the summer break had been over for a week already, the autumn training serials had started almost immediately, nobody knew it yet but tonight's training serial was going to be their last chance to exercise together for a long time, after this it was once again going to be for real.

Mike was looking forward to what should be an exhilarating if not long night, even when the boats were back in there was still a lot of work to do before the weekend could begin. This weekend would be especially good as there was going to be a wedding. A wedding was always a good crack, and everyone was looking forward to it.

There was however yet another long night to survive first it had taken them about an hour to transit from their base on the other side of Plymouth Sound to their current location in the large bay.

On route they had passed the mayflower steps where the Founding Fathers had left to colonize the New World, then under the lights of the Hoe, where in 1588 Sir Francis Drake had played his famous game of bowls before sailing out to battle the Spanish Fleet.

The 2 small black inflatable boats now sat 5 miles out in open sea waiting in the swell, everyone on board was a little tense, and all feeling a little weary after an hour of being battered and bounced through the waves, most of which were bigger than the boats. What they were about to do everyone had trained for, but this was the first time that the teams had tried the drills as part of a full exercise. For most of the troops on the boats it was there first time, they had all been briefed, and at first were excited by the prospect but now they didn't have much to do except sit, wait and think. There was a slight realisation and nervousness washing through the Commandoes, that was becoming more obvious but understandable. The deep dark swelling sea did not help the anxiety, 2 black pin pricks with only air, rubber and a few centimetres between them and the icy sea.

The craft rode the swell well now, the coxswains making small adjustments to keep them into weather. The boats would rise up gently, normally falling gently off the back of the moderate waves.

Occasionally as a larger swell would come, causing some concern to the passengers, as they spilled off of the tops of these larger waves, crashing in the troughs below.

The matt black inflatables were a new acquisition for the Marines; they had been a welcome change from the older more cumbersome craft that they had been used for several years. The single outboard engine was both reliable and powerful and the boat was very manoeuvrable. Due to its light construction it could also be paddled by the occupants, and used to drop off covert reconnaissance teams, and this stealth was what tonight was going to test.

Mike was feeling a little anxious himself, he was 100% sure he was in the right place, way out over to his left he could see the blinking light of the lighthouse, a bright white flash, twice every ten seconds reflecting off of the tops of the waves. This was the Eddystone, a group of Rocks that appeared out of the depths, 11 or 12 miles South West from Plymouth Breakwater.

Looking away and back now over the stern of the boat Mike saw the muddle of yellow and orange specs indicating lit houses and street lights, then the occasional glimpse of reds and greens as traffic lights changed. These were the lights of Looe, a small and picturesque Cornish Fishing Village, only a few miles away, and yet it seemed like another world, the world of normal people conducting their normal lives oblivious of what was happening just a couple of miles from their warm and cosy front rooms, or Pub lounges. Somewhere on the cliffs above the village two beams of light pierce through the night, and gave off a strange glow as the head lights of a car reflected off of some low cloud normally invisible in the dark.

The air was cold and blowing steadily into Mikes face as he looked forward again over the bow of the boat, Mike picked up his Night Vision scope and panned across the waves, they looked eerie in the false green light, Mike lowered the scope.

They had been only waiting a few minutes but it seemed like an age, nothing. he glanced across to Marco who had stationed his boat just off to his Starboard side, and gave an exaggerated shrug, it was returned in kind.

Then Mike, out of the corner of his eye, saw something glisten something was out of place in this sea of waves, he picked up his scope again, and looked across the left side of the boat, there it was, a slender tube appearing from the water. Wet and shining in the moon light, a small white wake forming behind the Periscope that they had been waiting patiently for. A little of Mikes anxiety lifted, at least they were all in the right place, he looked over at Marco and whistled pointing in the direction of the periscope, Marco nodded his understanding, and so Mike opened the throttle a little and began to follow the periscope which was still moving forward into the swell, slowly it began to rise higher out of the water, then an area of bubbling water appeared as the top of the sleek black conning tower appeared out of the water.

Mike manoeuvred his craft up behind the tower which was now at least a metre out of the water, behind him Marco had closed up and was following as close to Mikes boat as he dared, as the conning tower raised a little more the crews on the boats leant over and attached clips onto lines that had appeared just under the water, the crewman at the front of Mikes boat gave him a thumbs up and so Mike slowly released the throttle, the Zodiac sat back on the lines Mike happy with his position looked over his shoulder to check on Marco, within a few moments the other boat had settled also, Marco gave Mike a thumbs up. Mike using his torch flashed a pre arranged signal in the direction of the periscope, within a few seconds everything began to rise around him, the boat stopped floating as the sleek shape of the Submarine rose beneath them like a giant leviathan rising from the sea. Within a minute of the water washing off the decks figures appeared on top of the tower, one head looked down over the side, and gave a welcoming thumbs-up in the general direction of the boats.

Everything now began to happen as swiftly as a drill, this was why they had spent so much time training, Submariners dressed in dark water proof coats and life jackets appeared everywhere on the gently heaving deck, to take the equipment below, a tall Officer with his white roll up Jumper glowing brightly in the gloom guided the troops below, down through a small hatch, passing their weapons and gear down and into the warm environment of the Submarine.

Mike felt a tinge of jealousy knowing they were being led below to a bowl of Hot Broth and a home baked roll, meanwhile his guys had to stay out in the elements a little longer, as they stripped the boats down, hands and fingers began to numb as everything was wet, and the wind chilling.

The heavy outboard engines were removed from the stern of the craft, 3 men to an engine, cold hands trying to get a purchase on the metal bulk as they lifted it clear from the cold metal mounting plates, no easy task as they struggled not to slip on the wet deck, to drop and damage the propeller or lose it over the side, or worse still fall into the black swollen sea themselves.

With the help of the willing Submariners the boats were deflated and finally rolled up to be lowered by ropes below through a larger hatch and into the Submarine, everything just fitted.

Everyone was ordered below, Mike took one last look around just to be sure he hadn't forgotten anything, satisfied he climbed out of the icy wind and through the small hatch and down the grey ladder into the red light and warmth. He stopped in the small space to see the last Sailor come down the ladder, Mike watched with a nervous curiosity as he secured the hatch so that the massive 5000 tonne Submarine could be made water-tight and go where she was most comfortable, below the waves.

In the weapons space they had taken off their one piece black coxswain suits, and hung them on a line supported at one end by a frame that held a long sleek metal cylinder that was a live torpedo, Mike smiled and nudging Marco pointed at the other end that was tied off to an exercise bike!

Mike hung his ski goggles on the line that was also supporting a variety of woolly hats, gloves, and balaclavas, all steaming moisture in the warm air.

Breakfast at Babs'

Dressed in a green woolly jumper and damp combat trousers, Mike was now in a small corridor following Marco through the tight spaces that lead to the mess, squeezing past equipment, levers and pipes, he heard a sharp hiss of noise as the vents were opened and his ears popped as they slipped below the waves.

Marco looked back, 'look at all these buttons and switches, don't you just want to pull or turn something?'

'No I fucking don't!'

Mike sat down on a blue cotton covered bench seat, at a small white table big enough for 4, the table had a rectangular gold rubber place mat to stop anything slipping in bad weather.

One of the sailors placed a bowl of steaming soup and warm roll, in front of him

'there you go 'Royal'...enjoy'

Mike picked up a spoon, 'thanks mate' and smiled at Marco sat opposite 'this is the life eh'?

'sure is, better than I get at home' he smiled and looked over his shoulder for a moment, 'a few nervous faces around tonight' he was indicating towards a small cluster of the Marines that they had brought along for the Reconnaissance phase.

'Understandable really, we were all a bit nervous first time'

'not me' it was Col, Mikes signaller 'no worse than diving, I've been diving for years'

'yea muff diving, I always shit myself when I go down for the first time, ye never know what you're gonna to find!

'Crabs usually the sort of Muff you dive'

Mike laughed 'Fuckin alright give it a rest, I'm trying to eat my Broth'

Mike was just finishing his soup when the tall officer appeared at the door to the mess, still in his rolled up white sweater. 'Sergeant Cole, when your done you wanna come and chat to the skipper'

Mike was done anyway, 'yeah on my way, Sir'

'Were in the control room, you'll find it OK?'

'yeah no probs'

Mike went over to the Recce team leader, 'hey Knocker shall we go and see the skipper'

'do you know the way? It all looks the same to me!'

'yeah these things are all based on German U boats, I've seen Das Boot a hundred times, long thin and full of seaman, and the control room in the middle, easy!'

The pair walked through the cramped corridor and up to the control room, they had to squeeze past chairs occupied by sailors all manning computer screens, covered in various coloured lines.

Knocker was taking it all in for the first time, 'did you mean Das Boat, its more like Star Trek?'

In the centre was the captain, Mike had met him before, he was short with black and grey wiry hair, and just as he was now, he was always wearing a broad smile.

'Ah Sergeant, can't stay away eh?, thinking about joining the Navy?'

'Not on your life, I've seen the films you know'

'This is the Recce troop commander Corporal White'

Welcome onboard Corporal, enjoying your stay'

'5 star sir, better than the Ocean' HMS Ocean was an amphibious Helicopter carrier, and Knocker had flown from her into Iraq the year before.

'Ah yes well she's what we call a skimmer, or target, your much safer down here, now where do you want us to drop you off'

They all moved across to a chart table, the lines showed the position where they had been picked up. It also showed their current location about 10 miles out, and a box denoted the landing area marked Orange Beach.

Breakfast at Babs'

'Well the Lat and Long aren't exactly right some fool has just transferred them with a GPS from the grid reference, the beach is actually here'. Mike pointed with the tip of the pencil, and marked the landing site with an X.

'The tide is running out and the wind is Westerly, so I would like a drop off slightly East and about 6 Miles out, at 2145, about here is that possible?' Mike made a light lead circle on the chart.

The skipper looked past Mike, 'Navs, can we get the boys there?'

'yeah, I land you on the beach if you like!'

'not this time Navs' the skipper looked at Mike again, 'ah, yes, bounced off an uncharted sandbar a few weeks ago'

'Shit'

'Oh it happens occasionally, just skipped over it'

'yes no problem, well get into position from just after 2100, and you can come up and have a look at the beach on the periscope, then when you're ready well slip up and pop the hatches'

'Great thanks Sir, it'll be a shame to leave'

At 2107 Mike was asked to go back to the control room, he spent some time looking through the scope at maximum magnification, even at this range he could make out the features of the beach, it was only a small opening in the cliffs, surrounded by rocks, he could see the tale tale white tip as surf broke or waves hit rocks on the approaches. Behind he could see the dark cliffs that the recce team would have to climb.

Mike stepped out onto the hull of the Submarine; the wind was whipping spray over the top of the narrow deck. Submariners and Marines were busy preparing the boats for launch. He made his way down to his craft to check it over, checking for loose lines, and that all the equipment was once again secured to the deck and hull. He also checked that the wing nuts were tight where the engine was bolted to the stern. Mike looked at his compass, about the size of a hockey puck and secured on top of the tube the luminous tipped needle was swinging erratically confused by the mass of metal the boats were sat on.

Mike was content, and looked over to Marco, 'ready for the troops mate'

Marco nodded his checks also complete, 'Yep ready'

Col was positioned next to him, the radio was in a water proof rubber bag, it was strictly radio silence until the troops were secure on the beach so Col just helped Mike between monitoring his head set.

Knocker lead his team out, only 6 man strong, 2 would climb the cliff to secure it, 2 would prepare the ropes for the assaulting troops, who would land later, and the other 2 would remain on the beach to secure it, and lead the troops to the bottom of the ropes.

Knocker sat on the tube opposite Mike, no one was particularly happy about leaving the warm confines of the Submarine, with its endless supply of coffee, into the cold wet, winding night. Once they were away everyone would forget the comforts they had left behind and concentrate on the job in hand.

Everyone was loaded on, and the submariners had disappeared back down the hatch, Mike watched the red glow disappear as the hatch was closed and secured.

Alone on deck they waited, Mike flashed his torch at the periscope, a few seconds later a hissing noise signalled the air escaping from the huge beast as she once again slipped beneath the waves. Leaving the 2 craft suddenly tossing and lurching in the waves, once again pin pricks in an empty sea.

Mike lowered his engine, checked the lever was in neutral and half standing in the moving craft pulled the starter cord, almost falling on the wet deck in the process, the engine began to pop, splutter and smoke almost immediately, Mike recovered his balance.

Holding the tiller, and pushing the lever forward he turned the boat toward the dip in the cliff that Mike was using as a reference point for the beach. Mike checked his compass just to reassure himself that he was looking in the right direction, it should take 20 minutes to get to the point half a mile off of the beach where they would do a final check and prepare to land. There was no speedometer, the guys just used dead reckoning, and experience.

The swell was about 3 foot and following, so the coxswains had to control the boats so they didn't go too fast. Another consideration was keeping the boats wake to a minimum. Too much throttle and any enemy posted on the high cliffs would see a trail of bright white effervescence that would run unnaturally across the waves.

So far everything was going well, as usual the only real enemy was the weather, there was a saying in the amphibious world, when you were at sea you were never on exercise. The smallest problem compounded by a change in the weather, or an overloaded boat, or a commander that pushed the limits and took unnecessary risk could produce a life threatening incident within minutes, even within sight of a friendly shore.

However it was not uncommon for bad decisions to be made or advice ignored that could quickly produce the catalyst for such incidents. It was often the professionalism of the operators that made sure the line between pushing limits and personal disaster was so finely navigated, and exercised like this were where lessons should be learnt.

Tonight that possible catalyst was the stiff cold south-westerly breeze that was gradually building, the tops of the waves were beginning to foam. The freezing spray of water was hitting the blackened faces in the small rubber boats, everyone had the taste of salt on their lips, eyes were squinting, trying to read teh conditions ahead, but eyes were also wet with tears fighting off the stinging salt.

Even under the troops special protective suits the spray and windy conditions were making everyone wet and cold.

Mike eased the twist grip that was the throttle and slowed the boat to a stop. He turned the boat into the waves, Marco did the same and came around Mike so he was still sat off of Mikes port side.

Mike gave the hand signal to Marco for the FRV the final rendezvous point, Marco nodded and copied the signal back to confirm he understood.

The boats climbed the swell and tipped into the troughs conditions on board the craft were tight and it was hard to move around. As the craft fell over the waves the lads became almost weightless and had to hold on to something so that they didn't slip from the wet tubes that they were sat on.

Trying to adjust clothing, or even pull your wet woolly hat over your ears was a carefully planned manoeuvre.

Knocker locked his feet in under one of the straps that held the paddles in place, he pulled up his weapon and scanned the cliffs with his night sight.

Mike was looking over his shoulder at the beach 'Col get the Thermals out mate'

'You pouf its not that cold, and real commandoes don't wear underwear!' Mike just shook his head as Col chuckled and unzipped Mikes waterproof bag that was secured to the tube by metal karabiners. He reached inside and felt for the Thermal Imaging Camera.

Col switched on the camera and he too scanned

The beach and then the cliff, Knocker was looking up following the top of the cliff, 'Col, you see anything?'

'No, not on the beach, looks clear'

Knocker had seen a small flash of bright green through his sight, but was not sure what he had seen. 'Col you see the house left side of the dip in the cliffs'?

'Ah, hang on, yeah got it, I got a white hot plume from the chimney'

'OK come right about 200 mils, there's a lump on the hill, and something behind it I can't make it out, but looks too straight.'

Col scanned right, the picture was not as clear through the Thermal Imager as most of the cliff and hills behind were the same temperature. He stopped there was something odd, a few shapes were moving slowly across the cliff, he was about to say something then realised they were a little large and round, they were cows.

Then he saw the square shape, and through his camera he could just make out 3 plumes of white light.

'OK, I got something, 3 signatures, yep an engine block and 2 heads, its a Land Rover'

Knocker was trying to pick it out himself 'Shit, looking straight down on us'

Then one of the cows wandered in front of the square shape, Col watched as a line of heat appeared between it legs. 'Its OK I got a cow pissing between the wagon and us, the cows the same size as the Rover so it must be a well back from the edge, they won't see us…. see that Knocker'

'Yeah seen it' Knocker had seen a large flash of green light again, 'looks like they're too busy smoking, and that lighter would have killed their night vision, it doesn't look like they intend to be wandering anywhere near that cliff edge tonight'

Mike decided it was a good time to close on the beach 'right lets go then, no point waiting for their night vision to recover, Col bang them back in the bag for me mate'

'Roger'

Mike gave the signal and the 2 craft swung around and headed back towards the beach.

As the craft got closer the cliffs began to loom above them, the granite glowing white, in the moon light. Looking toward the landing site the moon was lighting the wave tops as they washed over the rocks, foaming and surging with luminescence.

With the noise of the waves they would be able to go in on engines, without being heard that would please everyone, especially the troops who were not fond of paddling.

Mike chose his rock it was about the right height and led onto a higher escarpment which looked ideal.

Mike quickly looked to his left to ensure Marco had enough space to find his own landing site.

Mike touched on and had to work hard to keep the boat under control against the rocks, and keep the stern straight so that he didn't end up smashed against the sharp rocks.

The recce team moved off one at a time, under Mike's direction, they looked back at him from the bows, and as he nodded they climbed over the front and scrambled onto the ledge.

Knocker tapped Mike on the shoulder, 'cheers mate, well have this rock marked when you come back'

'OK, take it easy' Mike was always felt a sense of relief when his boat was safely empty, the responsibility of driving a boat at night with all those sons of other mothers was considerable.

Mike was still glad he didn't have to do Knockers job, scaling that cliff in these conditions, then setting up ropes for 20 or 30 guys to scale was no mean feat, and he didn't really like heights anyway.

Mike reversed away from the rock, the swell smashed over the low stern as he did so and freezing cold water began to fill the small boat, sloshing around and making the small boat a little heavier and a little more unwieldy. Mike turned as soon as he was far enough away and drove out through the waves again. The water gradually emptied out through the outlets in the mounting plate below his engine.

Mike led the two boats back out, searching the wave tops for the dark shape of a larger craft, sat somewhere in another rendezvous point was the small landing craft that held the rest of the Marines. This consisted of a troop of 20 men who were to attack the Radar installation.

Mike had seen it through the submarine periscope sitting on top of the white granite cliff and barely silhouetted against the moonless night sky.

Mike saw the silhouettes of the 2 small landing craft as they appeared and disappeared on the waves. They would have to give knocker 2 hours to set up, and it was an hour round trip, so they would have time for a coffee and something to eat.

As they got closer Mike could pick out the guys standing on the deck waiting to receive their lines and tie them on. He could also see the other 3 inflatable's like ducks in a row being towed behind their mother craft.

Mike pulled alongside the steel Landing Craft, the coxswain was running it away from the sea to make things easier, but trying not to run too far and so closer to the land and danger.

On the deck a tall figure was waiting, Col leaned forward and coiled up the bow line, he threw it up to waiting hands. Now secure on the bollard Mike threw over the stern line and secure turned off the engine, and pulled it up out of the water.

'About time mate, all the bacon butties are almost gone and there's a hot wet on' Sven offered Col a hand and hauled him from the boat, Mike was then offered a hand and followed.

The hatch at the rear of the troop canopy was open and steam was coming from the compartment, inside were 10 of the assault troops, they were mostly asleep, a couple were at the back heating up a meal from their rations. The boil in the bag meals were in a silver square foil packet and were OK if you could get more than 2 different menus in a week's period it was not unusual to have meatballs and pasta for 2 or 3 days without a change, the other problem was one per meal was never enough.

Marco had secured his boat on the port side and appeared at the hatch, 'room for a little one'

Jon was by the steaming kettle, 'plenty of room, come on in and join the party'. Marco stepped down behind Mike he was the section second in command but was only a lance corporal, this meant that although he was mature and bright enough, he had not pushed himself up the promotion ladder as yet and although everyone knew he was capable enough, he was not allowed to take on the responsibility of this kind of task, which would normally be given to a Corporal to command. Mike as the Sergeant would usually have found himself commanding the amphibious element of the operation as a whole, and should really have been sat in one of the Landing Craft co-ordinating, but manpower was so short at the moment and commitments were so great they had to just make things work as they went along.

Mike was sure Marco would move on soon, he had too, he was married now, and with a baby on the way would soon need the extra pay. In the mean time Mike relished the opportunity to lead from the front again, and get hands on at the coal face.

As Sven descended the short metal ladder Jon filled another mug, 'how was the sub?'

'The broth was fuckin lush, but no chicks!' moaned Marco, stepping over the sleeping body of one of the Marines.

'Ah well you cant have a woman running around a smarty tube with live Tomahawks and Nukes on PMT!'

'Fair one, that time of the month with the missus and a shopping trolley in Asda is like a fuckin nuclear war!'

Jon handed a steaming plastic thermal mug to Mike, 'have a coffee mate, do you want any scran, we got bacon butties?

Mike wasn't hungry 2 bowls of thick soup and as much fresh bread as you could eat had quashed any appetite he had, 'No thanks mate'

Jon handed Col a mug, 'what's the beach like?'

Breakfast at Babs'

'Well, you might as well get everyone together and I'll give you a heads up, might as well grab the troop commander, and section commanders in as well'

Mike had the lads all huddled around a map, a chart and an aerial photo.

'OK guys almost as we planned and rehearsed, just one change Boss, the beach has far too much surf, and its too tight, so you will be landing over rocks, just remind the guys that no one gets off without getting the nod from the coxswain, we don't want any broken ankles, or worse'

The troop commander was a young lieutenant, probably his first amphibious exercise with just his troop and seemed to be enjoying the challenge 'No worries Sergeant'

It was not long after Mike finished his brief that it was time to get ready to move off, they pulled in the boats that were strung out over the stern, and the coxswains began to start their engines, and lose from the tow.

The craft all sat in lines behind their respective landing craft, waiting to be called forward to load the troops, Mike watched as one of the 3 man crew waved at him and pointed to the Port side of the larger boat.

Mike manoeuvred his craft over the stern wake and onto the starboard side to load up the troops; he knew that Marco in boat 2 was doing the same on the port side.

Keeping the small inflatable alongside at night in these conditions was not easy, the troops sensed the tension, and realised by the movement of the craft that this was not an evolution without its dangers.

The small boats were lurching and bouncing alongside the larger steel landing craft. The Marines lowered first their small day sacks containing their equipment, and one at a time lowered themselves, waiting for the swell to lift the smaller craft up and closer, so that the drop to negotiate was only a metre or so into the tiny craft, to jump in would have been extremely dangerous, and even bounce you out and into the waiting sea.

Once loaded Mike nodded at the landing craft crewman, he then checked over his shoulder and pulled away and out into the swell. Mike lay off to the stern of the two landing craft again and watched as the rest of the boats loaded up and joined him from where he would lead them all onto the landing site.

The approach was slow, Col was directing looking through a Night Vision monocle and using the infra red markers that now flashed invisibly to the naked eye, but now marked Mikes original rock he guided them towards the beach.

The boats landed once again, holding the bow on to the rock, Mike watched as the troops struggled to clamber up and over the slippery rocks with their weapons and equipment, the deepening swell off shore was making things even more dangerous amongst the rocks, every now and again Mike had to stop the guys and adjusting the throttle, and using the tiller he struggled to make it as safe as he could. Finally the last guy was off, a glance at Marco told him he was also empty and ready to retreat, the landing site was only big enough for 2 boats at a time, so Mike and Marco pulled away, and sat off watching as the other craft delivered their load of troops.

When they were all complete Mike gave everyone a thumbs up and began the long transit home.

It was a rough ride back with no weight in the craft, and worst of all into the elements, Mike thought it would take at least an hour to clear the headland and get into the shelter of the sound. The coxswains were used to the hard ride, with feet locked in under paddles, or equipment, and holding tight with cold and wet gloved hands was no easy task. Mike winced as his spine gave him a sharp pain every time the boat fell off the top of a big crest, his eyes strained into the wind as he tried to pick out features to navigate by.

Breakfast at Babs'

They eventually reached the jetty, a few of the guys had come down to help them tie on, after shifting his kit onto the large concrete pontoon, Mike stood upright and straight for the first time in about 2 hours, he felt a little un balanced as his brain tried to tell him he was still on a moving boat. Mike was a little under 6 ft tall, his stocky frame hidden for the moment under the black one piece waterproof suit, and green life jacket, Mike first took off his gloves, and then his soaking wet black woolly hat, running a hand through his very wet short dark hair, he placed both hands on his lower back and leaned over backwards, 'Jesus Marco, I'm glad that's over my backs fucked'

Marco held his right wrist in his left hand, 'mines OK, but my wrist is hanging out from the throttle'

'you need to play with yourself more often, it's good for the wrist muscles'

'Don't need too, I got a missus for that!' Marco winked.

'Yeah right'

'Yeah fair one, I do tend to do it myself' Marco shrugged

Mike stood and watched the other boats coming in, grabbing lines and helping move kit up onto the jetty.

Mike had been a Royal Marine for 16 years; he had joined just before the end of the cold war. Then you were still taught about the USSR and the threat of the great Russian Bear, the huge number of Tanks, Aircraft and Infantry Fighting Vehicles massed on the Borders of Eastern Europe poised to attack the capitalist west.

The frightening possibility of battle field Biological and Chemical weapons, specialist Russian night fighters who only worked and trained at night.

Mike had since met a Czechoslovakian Tank Commander, who had told him of how his tanks would have once been in the vanguard of any attack on NATO's forces in Europe, Mike still found it strange that this former enemy, now a Colonel, worked for NATO in one of the most sensitive buildings in the world.

In the early days the Royal Marines spent every winter in Norway, the stalwart of NATO's protection of the 'Northern Flank' it was a traditional battleground for the corps, many of the first Commando raids had been carried out in places like Tromso, and Narvik, 200 miles inside the Arctic Circle. Many of the first foreign commando's were brought back as volunteers after raids on some of the remote towns and fishing villages. Mike had a great respect for men such as the Telemark Hero's who had spent months surviving in the extreme conditions, evading the Germans before destroying the Heavy Water Plant at Rjukan, so delaying the Germans attempts at producing their own hydrogen Bomb.

The days of Communism were now past and as the wall fell in the west, Kuwait was invaded by Iraq, and once again the Middle East was seen as the next melting pot.

Even Northern Ireland was starting to de-escalate, Mike had accumulated 2 years in the 90's and left for the final time in 2000, once the training ground of the British forces, now too tied up in politics, there was no longer the money in being a terrorist in the republic, running drugs, booze or petrol and the occasional bank robbery was a more lucrative way of life.

Mike had been giving a lecture when the world changed again on September 11th, suddenly the Americans had to learn over night what the British had learnt over 2 World Wars and 30 years of efforts by the IRA when its citizens had stood against Zeppelin bombers, the nightly Blitz, the threat of invasion, or innocent people being blown apart at memorial services giving thanks to those that had already sacrificed their tomorrows.

Mikes view was a simple view but that's all soldiers like him needed to form his political opinions, no point making it too complicated.

He understands the feelings in his own soul, and of those around sitting in the same filthy hole, he knew the difference between a worthy cause and getting someone more votes, but he did'nt really care. He also knew that when the time comes its all about looking after those round you and hoping they look after you.

Most importantly it was making sure everyone made it so they can all laugh about it in the Pub afterwards.

Now that the oldest excuse to fight had come back to the fore, Religion, and terrorism had found its way to America it was suddenly a world concern, Afghanistan, Iraq, or was it oil, all he knew is the cost of petrol wasn't going down and neither were the mortgage payments on his 2 bedroom house in Dorset.

There was a famous poster during the Second World War of a merchant sea man laying dying on a piece of drift wood in the middle of the Atlantic, behind him his oil tanker is slipping beneath the waves, recently torpedoed by a U boat and the caption read something like 'Petrol prices to increase by 1 pence'. Nothing changes.

Still its what he'd joined the Corp for, the excitement of being up there on the front line where ever it was, he'd served 3 tours in Northern Ireland seen it when it was bad, then later through the peace process, seen the activities become more criminal. Using the conflict as a cover for bigger profits, sure the guy in the street with a balaclava was still the same old paddy who had fought the 'English' since the days of William of Orange, but he was now more of a puppet than ever, and just like the common British soldier would never get rich from it.

Mike had also deployed to Northern Iraq helping protect the Kurds in the aftermath of the 1st Gulf War, they had spent nearly 2 months living in villages, helping those that had been victimised by Hussein and his henchman. They had cleaned out the Iraqi secret police and sent them packing, removed the car batteries and electrodes and washed out the blood from the torture cells in school basements. Then when it was time to withdraw there was no-one to relieve them, no UN or Peacekeepers ,

35

the people knew they were being fed back to the wolves, they protested and pleaded not to be left without protection. They had pulled out anyway, no reason to stay any longer the Kuwait oilfields were no longer burning.

The Kurds had received a little humanitarian aid, it had all looked good to the people at home, sitting down to their Supper with a clear conscience, so as quickly as they had arrived they all packed and left, leaving them to their fate, the vacuum undoubtedly filled with Iraqis with a score to settle.

The story had been the same for years, Cambodia, Sierra Leon, Afghanistan, the list was endless, but it kept Mike and guys like him in a job, and made things a little interesting, there was never any point looking too deeply into it you just drew your salary, spent it on beer and enjoyed life while you still could.

The World would continue to change and so would priorities, today's priority was to get ready for a Wedding.

Chapter 2
Jerusalem

It was the usual pre Wedding morning, up too late with a banging hang over, boots still to polish and trying to remember what you'd done the night before.

Mike crawled out of his single bed got his feet tangled and fell over the pink trousers that were laying on the floor. A blurred vision and memories slowly returned to him, piece meal and in small chunks of realisation.

The dance floor of the Academy, the girl who teased him and called him fat then the challenge to exchange clothes, the pink trousers were a tight fit. The only way to get them on was by splitting the seams with a set of keys supplied by Gris, then with Jon's boot laces cut in half, tied together up the sides of his thighs. It had been a real team effort, but what a way to lose a 50 quid pair of jeans and then still wake up alone.

Mike picked up his watch from the top of the telly, 10:30, shit, better have a coffee and try to sober up.

Mike lived in the barracks, near to the city, in a small one man cabin, the size of a child's room, but adequate enough for his needs. It overlooked

37

the car park, and the morning light streamed in through a sash window. Against one wall was a small single bed, with a thick horse hair mattress, and an old Thunderbirds themed quilt on top. Against the opposite wall were beach effect fitted wardrobes with a desk in the middle, above which was a small pin board covered with pictures of his family. His mum sitting on a wooden stile in a field behind her house, next to her sat a black Newfoundland dog, a Polaroid of his younger sister in her first car, a small pink Corsa, she had sent it to him when he had been in Ireland, on the back it read, 'look out Mikey this chicks pink, fast and mobile... xx'

Even though the room was small Mike had managed to get a few luxuries into it, the most useful of which was a small beer fridge which sat on the window ledge of the white tiled en suit bathroom. The fridge was full of beer, cans, bottles, a couple of chocolate bars from unused ration packs and a carton of milk, the wire led out on an extension to a plug in the main cabin.

Mike pushed the button on the small kettle that sat on top, and stumbled to the sink.

He leaned with his hands on both sides of the sink, looking at himself through bleary eyes, 'Jesus I look like shit' Mike liked talking to himself, it made things seem more definite, even if he had thought things through first he sometimes had to repeat them out loud, 'where do I start' he laughed to himself, 'I know' and picked up his razor.

It took 3 mugs of coffee, and about an hour before Mike felt clear-headed enough to begin preparing his uniform.

He sat in front of the TV watching a Saturday morning kids show, and polished his boots. The TV was another small luxury, it was only a 14 inch portable, but had once been the families first colour TV. He had had it for his whole career, and it was still going strong, the only problem these days was even though he only got to watch it a few times a year everyone had to have a TV licence. Even though it was small it was solid state, so it was a heavy thing to hide very time he went away!

Mikes taxi pulled up outside the Spy Glass, the Pub was directly opposite from the church and the best place for the lads to meet and warm up for a good old sing song in the pews

The guys all looked smart in their number 1 'Blues' uniform, brass belt buckles shinning, and plastic belts and caps bright white, there was something about a Bootneck wedding.

Col walked in with his wife, 'what's going on here, a bus conductor's reunion!'

Marco tapped Mike on the shoulder,

'Guinness, Mate?'

'yeah cheers mate'

'Hey Mike, have you met Cath, me missus, this is Mike, the bossy fucker I told you about'

Cath was slim 5'7, 25, and had one of those impish faces that suited the shinning black bob that was holding up that 'wedding only' accessory the straw hat. Caths was adorned with the obligatory huge yellow sunflower.

A tall blond figure moved across to the group it was Sven, so named because his last name was Hazel, which is almost like Hassel! and since he is blond he was named after the German soldier and novelist. 'hey guys a wedding in rig eh, the best way to trap a bird, only just better than dressing up as a woman, or in her pink trousers eh Mike!

'Ah yeah, I m still not sure I have the whole story worked out yet, good night though, I think, I just need another trip away now, and save up for another pair of Levi's'

Sven leaned in, 'any more buzzes Mikey?'

As Mike spoke everyone listened, they had all been wanting to ask the same question 'no not yet, just the usual question about how long we'd need to prep, and how much kit we'd need'

'How long did you tell them, about 9 months would be good, I'll be on drafted somewhere new in 8' it was Col, Cath had been ordering the drinks but heard the conversation 'what's that Colin, your not going away again?, you lot only just got back!' it was Mike who answered as honestly as he could, but trying not to upset her and maybe spoil the day for them both ' we don't know anything yet, but were all on call, its better than the lads from 45 Commando in Afghanistan, they've already been out there for 3 months and wont be home for Christmas, if we do go to Iraq it will only be for a short tour' he laughed it off, 'you know the saying, the war'll be over before Christmas'

The day went well, they took up the last 2 rows of pews in the small church, the first hymn was a struggle, no-one really knew how it should go, neither apparently did the organist. Everyone was still as the Royal Marines prayer was read

O Eternal Lord God, who through many generations hast united and inspired the members of our Corps,
Grant thy blessings we beseech thee, on Royal Marines serving all round the globe.
Bestow Thy crown of righteousness upon all our efforts and endeavours, and may our laurels be those of gallantry and honour, loyalty and courage.
We ask these in the Name of Him whose courage never failed, our redeemer Jesus Christ

It was then time for every Englishman's favourite, 13 uniformed voices of various talents most of them tone deaf, singing as if it was the last night of the 'proms' or a 6 nations final at Twickenham, Jerusalem was always a hymn everyone thought they could sing well!

Everyone had noticed the cute bridesmaids all in pink on the front pew, she was tall slim and very blonde, as the singing reached its peak she looked around to see where the croaking noise was coming from, Mike caught her eye, and saw her giggle before she looked back hiding the giggles in her Hymn sheet.

The photos took forever, all the grannies wanted their pictures taken with the Marines, some of the lads had already sneaked back to the pub, and it wasn't long until the bar was again stacked with a tower of white peak caps with red bands, and glasses filled. With Cath gone to chat in the corner with Gris's girlfriend the subject turned back to Iraq, 'so come on Mike how long did you give us?'

Mike replied quietly so as not to upset the girls '48 hours to prep kit and then leave for Brize 4 days max', Brize Norton was the RAF airbase close to Oxford.

Gris leaned in 'does that include time to sober up!'

'You'll never be sober' retorted Col.

Everyone laughed, the conversation needed a quick change of direction as the girls headed back towards the group, 'hey did you hear about the lads in 40 Commando, I saw Jan Roberts last weekend just back from Iraq, anyway you know Jan'

Yeah Jan the man, he's got a Dick on him even Cath couldn't fit in her gob'

Cath gave Col a sharp elbow to the stomach,

'Fit in yours though wouldn't it Col love'

When the laughing had stopped Griz carried on with his tale, 'ye the story goes that Toni Blair visited the lads just before they came back, went around all the usual places, all the lads got told not to drip or tell it how it really is, you know the usual shit, anyway he gets to meet one of the teams as it comes back from patrol, obviously they've really been waiting around the corner for an hour, anyway the Land Rovers pull up, all the lads jump off to have a chat with him, CO, RSM and all the usual officers are there watching and listening, anyway all the young lads are playing the game, towing the party line and he comes to Jan and his mate, asks them

41

something about the mail getting through or whatever, Jan says to the Prime Minister, 'Sir do you mind doing a photo?' so the camera comes out of Jans Webbing, Toni Blair says of course not, it would be a pleasure, so what does Jan do, gives the Prime Minister his fuckin disposable £2.99 camera, say's 'just press that button on top Sir' grabs his oppo and poses'

'Whoofin' cries Col laughing at the image of the Prime Minister taking a photo of the guys 'does he do it'

'Yea Jan's got this picture of his mate and him all tooled up, grinning like kids, trying not to laugh, as the fuckin Prime Minister takes their picture on a Boots throw away camera.

As the noise of the infectious crescendo of laughter filled the Pub, Mike headed for the toilet and looked back at the guys, it was times like these that made the bad times all disappear, and everyone got the feeling that they were part of something special.

The call came on Sunday morning, it was the unit second in command, 'sorry to spoil your Weekend sergeant, can't say too much over the phone but PJHQ have given the go ahead they want you to fly out before the end of the week, I'll give you all the info tomorrow', only the timing was a surprise, it was a little quicker than he thought, Mike moved out into the corridor to be out of ear shot of the girl wearing his England Rugby shirt laying in his single bed.

'Right' O Sir, I'll see you in the morning, we've got a lot to do!' he pressed the end call button, shit, a lot to do that was an understatement, however time for that later, shame not to take advantage of a horny young ex bridesmaid laying in his bed. She was still half asleep, but began to respond to the tender touch of Mike's fingers tracing her nipples under the no 7 shirt. The call was all but forgotten as he moved between her tanned thighs and began to tease her to another orgasm, he was smiling inside as he made the girl buck with his tongue moving to the tune of Jerusalem echoing in his minds ear.

Chapter 3
Deployment

Mike pulled through the gates at the base, the security guard smiled a good morning, and waved him through, as he pulled up he glanced over to where the boats were moored. Alongside a floating pontoon there were several Rigid Raiding craft, with their flat hulls and powerful engines they could carry raiding troops at over 30knots. Delivering them swiftly onto a beach, or silently into enemy lines they were painted in a dazzle paint scheme that worked equally well in Norway or Plymouth. Tied to the outside of these, smaller and lower in the water were the black hulls of the inflatable's, Mike looked at them for a moment and wondered if they had never looked so vulnerable to him before.

Mike climbed the stairs that lead to the changing rooms and found the 'tea boat', this was a small room next to the locker room set aside for the lads to relax and take a coffee break. Marco was just sitting down with a coffee on an old red settee. Just like the fridge and the TV it had been rescued from the skip, in the chair next to him one of the other lads, Gris was leaning over polishing his black boots.

Gris was a short stroppy blonde haired Gordie, he was one of Mikes 3 Corporals, and so was a section commander, responsible for 5 or 6 boats. Gris had worked for Mike for the last year, and was a young and keen professional who Mike relied on for a lot of the tasking.

Above where Gris sat the wall was covered with flags and photos, all souvenirs of past exercises and operations. Each flag was signed by the guys that had been in the troop for that particular trip, and below most a collection of digital photographs recounting events, some pictures of groups, some with scenery typical of the country. Snowy mountains, camels, rolling surf, there was a new photo on the wall blown up to A4 and slightly grainy, it was of 2 guys in desert camouflage and weapons next to a Land Rover, the caption was scrawled rather than written in red crayon and read, *Foto by Toni blur, Prime Inister of Britin, ageb 47½..*

Below the White on Red Norwegian cross there were shots of Mike and Marco in Norway Ski-ing across a frozen lake with white mountains forming the sharp back drop, another of Sven breaking through chunks of Fjord ice in his hard hulled Rigid Raiding craft.

On the opposite wall above the fridge was the frayed Stars and Stripes that had flown from one of the American gunboats that had supported the Squadron in the last Iraq War. These craft had been manned by Navy SEAL's who had become very close to their British counterparts and there were dozens of photo's of brothers in arms surrounding the tattered edges.

'Where's the rest?

Gris replied, 'where else, in Babsies, watching Sven filling his huge hole, it's the morning ritual!'

'Babs' canteen, was almost as old as the squadron itself and had been run for as long as anyone could remember by 2 local ladies, Barbara and Carole, who had provided the lads with moral lifting Tea, Coffee, and hot

Pasties and Bacon Rolls at all times of the day or night. They had shared the good and the bad times alongside the lads, and had seen its members come and go.

'OK come on then well all go for a coffee and I'll give you the 'good news'

'Shit don't tell me were off to the Caribbean to soak up the sun guarding the Jamaican girls beach volley ball team on a visit to a rum distillery' Gris rose from the settee

'Close, it'll be sunny, and plenty of sand!' Mike smiled

He led them through to the canteen, on the way they passed the Commanding Officer, as he pushed open the fire door with his shoulder, struggling to balance his Bacon Buttie on top of his mug of tea, holding his briefcase in the other, 'Ah Morning Sergeant Cole, can you come and see me when your ready'

'Aye Sir, be 10 minutes or so, just gotta brief the lads'

'No rush, when you're ready'

Mike entered the Canteen, on the wall was a TV showing a string of children's programs, at the moment the Teletubbies were rolling around their grassy hill side. The news only got a look in if the female presenter was good looking, and Natasha Kaplinski was on holiday at the moment.

Sven was sat munching on a breakfast bap whilst watching Tinkey Winkey making tubby toast. The white bun overflowing with brown sauce and a full English breakfast that would normally have filled a plate, the lads took seats around the table. Mike was stood at the counter 'anyone for Coffee' everyone except Sven and Marco took up the offer.

Stood awaiting his order was Carole, a middle aged women who had run the canteen with Babs for as long as anyone could remember, she had been born and bred in the local area, and her strong West country accent was often the brunt of a few jokes and a favourite for mimic takers , '6 coffee's please Carole'

'You paying cash Mike', a laugh came from inside the fridge, Babs was getting more bacon out, the Scottish accent still unmistakable even after 20 odd years down South 'Mike, cash, you gotta be joking, he hasn't paid cash since he conned his ex girlfriend into paying his bill at Families Day'

'Hey she was a modern girl and it was her turn to buy the meal, and I knew I was gonna bin her, so it was my last chance' Mike shrugged

'Anyway you heard the lady, tab it is, I'll pay by the end of the week, Friday OK?'

Yeah we've heard that one before Babs, haven't we?, knowing you its cause you're going away Thursday!'

Babs came from the fridge, 'well you aint leaving the country'

Mike smiled, 'not for a few days at least'

As the banter continued around him, Mike looked around him. Apart from a few prints of famous landscapes over the wall, there was only one other object on the wall, there mounted in a glass and wood frame was a photo and a pair of boot laces, Chris had been the Units only fatal casualty in Iraq so far and everyone hoped the last, the boot laces had come form a kit sale. A tradition in the Royal Marines, if you died in service an Auction was held and all of your belongings from your locker were sold off. All the money raised was given to the Wife or Parents, normally guys formed syndicates and pooled money. The smallest and most ridiculous items usually went for extortionate amounts of money, Mike had seen boot laces taken from their boots go for 50 quid and the boots themselves go for hundreds of pounds. Let's hope they didn't have to have a kit sale this year.

Mike gave out the coffee's and sat at the top of the table, he had not been around for the invasion of Iraq, the first Operation Tellic, the War that was apparently over, but a lot of the guys now sitting in front of him had.

'OK, everyone around this table will be flying out at the end of the week, Gris you'll be the section commander and my 2ic'

Breakfast at Babs'

Gis nodded, he had already volunteered his services as Mikes 2nd in command, he was keen to get a break from his Wife, 'cool, that will please the missus'

Mike continued, 'I don't know much about the task yet, but I should find out some more when I see the CO after this, the only thing I really know is that well take 6 Zodiacs, and well be working in the Marsh and lake areas bordering Iran, about half way between Basrah and Baghdad.'

'When we flyin?'

'Friday, we'll fly from Brize on Friday about midday', there was a silence around the room as everyone took in what had been said, then the questions came, firstly the usual about how long they could expect to be away, would they get any time to get home to the family, then the discussion turned to the equipment and stores that would be required, and it became obvious they weren't as prepared as they thought.

'OK we better get crackin, but how about this, if we get into any trouble anyone that gets themselves wounded, gets everyone a full English breakfast here the day we get back'

Sven looked over his bap, 'happy with that'

As he stood Mike hit the table, 'right let's do it then'

The Commanding Officer of the unit was very approachable and obviously enjoyed commanding the unit. He commanded, as he would tell anyone at the drop of a hat the only operationally deployable boat unit in the British armed forces.

Mike was invited into the office, and sat himself down opposite the large desk, a humming noise and diesel smell was coming from the open window behind the Colonel, Mike knew it was from a large coaster that had just arrived alongside the commercial jetty opposite.

'So Sgt Cole happy that the uncertainty's over' Mike nodded but was thinking in the back of his mind that the uncertainty was probably about to begin, 'yes Sir, but do we know what we are actually going to be doing?'

'only what you already know, an anti smuggling op in support of the ground forces on the border, were waiting for a more in depth brief, the Operations Officer will let you know when it arrives'

'I realise it doesn't give you much time, we will of course send you off with as much support as you need, go see Ops in a minute and get a copy of the brief, the whole Squadron is here so use them, and if there's anything you cant get in the usual way let me know, happy?' it was obvious that the meeting was over,

'yeah reasonably, cheers Sir' Mike rose to leave

'and how about the Lads, they keen?'

'itching Sir' just like me Mike almost added as he walked out his mind now beginning to race, he began to think of all the jobs that needed doing to get them away at such short notice.

Mike popped in to see the Operations Officer; they had joined the unit on the same day 2 years before, and had become good friends.

Mike knocked on the open door and walked in to the office, 'OK boss?'

'ah Mike, come in take a seat, I don't have much for you unfortunately, the brief is not very detailed, we asked for more info but it never materialised, the CO is going to try to talk on a secure link later to someone in the brigade out there, but I still don't reckon you'll get anything useful until you're face to face, and they are Army so may not really understand what you can do yet'

'Same old, same old then' Mike leaned back in the chair.

'I'm afraid so, but anything else I can do let me know, I wish I was coming with you'

'Yeah I know, but who's going to keep this lot running, OK I better get the lads in gear, cheers boss'

The week would be spent collecting equipment, firing on the range, and preparing all the equipment to fly.

Breakfast at Babs'

They would be flying out on Friday so there wasn't much time left, and the hardest part of deploying anywhere in the world was getting through Brize Norton.

At Brize Norton it had been the usual bureaucracy trying to emplane with all the kit, especially the empty fuel bags. The bags were large rubber sausages that were each designed to carry 25 litres of petrol, there were 40 bags in all, most were brand new and had never seen a drop of petrol, but that didn't concern the RAF. They had started by packing them in wooden packing crates, Mike thought that this would please the Air force staff, but they were then told it had to go in special cardboard boxes. The RAF didn't have any so Mike had spent about an hour phoning around various people in various units trying to find some.

After receiving a call from his own Unit saying that they couldn't get any, and with about 2 hours until the flight Mike turned to the young female corporal who the lads had nicknamed, Helga 'what are so special about these cardboard boxes, they water proof or fuel proof or something'

The girl was really starting to piss everyone off, she was enjoying her little power play with this 'cocky bunch of guys who thought they were tough'

'No just normal but they got a black diamond stamped on the side that says UN and a serial number for petrol'

Mike looked around at the lads, then back at the Corporal, 'your joking right?'

'No of course not, everything has to be done by the book'

'are you fuckin pissed, show me' Mike grabbed a pot of pens from the desk where he was stood, he tipped them out all over the tidy desk, grabbing a black indelible marker he threw it at the girl, 'show me, on one of those boxes'

The girl jumped, she was only about 20, but she'd played her games with the wrong crowed. Timidly she drew a black diamond and through the centre wrote in large figures on the crate, UN1203.

Mike watched arms folded leaning in the doorway between the office and the hangar, 'is that it? right looks like we have our boxes then, OK Sven grab a pen'

The girl stood up, she was nearly in tears, 'you cant do that, I'm going to phone my Flight Sergeant'

With a load cry of 'ooooow' and the lads pretending to hold handbags up to their chests, the girl ran off to the phone, for a brief moment Mike felt a little awkward for the girl, and then laughed.

After a few minutes a flight Sergeant came in, dressed in the light blue of the RAF, he was so tall he had to duck through the door, he held a hand out to Mike, and smiled under a grey handle bar moustache, Mike smiled as he accepted his hand, 'hi mate, I'm Clive Watson, what's the problem'

Mike explained the box situation, pointing towards the wooded crates, explaining the frustrations and the importance of the equipment flying to Iraq without delay, Clive picked up the paperwork, and producing a pair of half moon spectacles began to studied it, leafing through the sheets stone faced. Mike was imagining Clive Watson in his peak cap, the Bus Inspector type, or maybe a traffic warden, Mike could only imagine what hoops and hurdles would need to be jumped through next.

Clive looked up and placed his glasses on his head, 'OK I'm sorry you have been messed about, I'm afraid Corporal Wilson is a little rigid'

Mike heard a whisper in the background; he didn't need to hear anyone say 'frigid' to know what the childish giggling was about. If Clive heard the comment he ignored it and carried on non-perplexed 'You've filled all the paperwork as an operational move'

'Well yea, were off to Iraq'

'Ok but if we change it to a training manifest, then your good to go, no need for the cardboard boxes'

'Your Joking, that simple, but operational shit should be easier than moving training gear'

Clive shrugged, 'welcome to the RAF, that's the way it is'

Mike then realised all the mountains of paperwork he had done, 'so I've got to destroy another rain forest and do all that again'

Clive smiled, 'no, not you', he turned to the desk, 'Lu Lu come over here and get all this retyped on to a 131'

Lu Lu had that look of a school girl being told off by the teacher, if she had been chewing bubble gum she would have blown a bubble right about now.

'OK Sarge' she glared at Mike, so Mike turned to Clive and offered his hand, 'many thanks mate, shame you cant thrash them around the parade ground with their weapon above their heads'

Clive smirked, 'Not like the good old days eh!'

Mike walked out of the office where all the lads were still giggling, ' 'let's go and eat shall we?

As they walked back to the transit parked outside the hangar someone began to whistle a tune at the crescendo of which everyone yelled 'Shout!...come on now....Shout!'

The departure procedure for anyone flying with the RAF was loosely based on that used in any civilian airport, the departure lounge was more akin to what Heathrow must have looked like when it began flying on the first transatlantic crossings with Comet Passenger Jets.

The lounge had a variety of museum furniture. The more comfortable looking seats were straight backed and covered in dark green PVC, the less comfortable ones were plastic bucket seats and every fourth pair had a small wire table welded between them.

The departure lounge was already busy with passengers mostly dressed in Desert Fatigues. Here and there were also servicemen with their families probably flying back to postings in Germany or Cyprus.

Normally Mike would have been quite jealous, watching other people going about normal daily activities, when you were just about to go away for a long time it often made it harder. This time however Mike looked around him, and thought that people should be jealous of him, he was glad he was flying out to Iraq, and in charge of such a professional team of guys, the adrenalin was really pumping through him.

Someone stepped out in front of the crowd of varying uniforms, he was wearing a half open, creased combat jacket and without making any attempt to introduce himself started shouting 'Right you lot, there's no smoking in the terminal, you can smoke over in the corner by the toilets, there's no smoking out by the entrance, if I catch anyone they can clean up all the butts that are out there, right any questions?'

Mike looked at the others' Scruffy, arrogant Prick'

Sven raised his hand, the Sergeant looked over, and pointed, everyone looked towards Sven, who in the tone of a dim-wit but with a subtle twist of sarcasm asked

'Hello Sergeant, where can I have a fag?'

Everyone laughed, the Sergeant tried to say something in reply but was lost, seeing defeat in the face of a bunch of Royal Marines who would only heckle him into submission, he walked away.

The next guest speaker was a short dumpy female, this time dressed in the light blue uniform of the RAF, with a Navy blue skirt, 'Can I have your attention please, my name is Corporal Green, I must remind you that you are not allowed to board the aircraft with any sharp objects, this includes any knives and scissors, please come forward and hand in any of these items now'

The guys all returned to the circle that they had formed besides a large glass cased model of a Hercules quite obviously as old as the furniture that it complimented so well.

Gris began the conversation, 'I fuckin hate this place who was that bolshie wanker, no one needs to be talked to like that, at least the chick was OK'

Breakfast at Babs'

'Fuck me Gris, OK?' Sven was not going to let that comment go, 'Compared to what? We haven't even left the UK yet and you've lowered your standards'

'Well mate, as I always say aim low, and your never disappointed! You should try it sometime might not have to spend so much money on Franky Vaughn!'

'Yeah Swedish Male porn!' injected Mike

Sven turned to Mike 'Yeah right mate, you know I don't want everyone to know I'm a porn star. Anyway that was the same bird from when we flew out to Norway, you remember, she came round with a bag, asked us to hand in our knives, forks and spoons'

'No way?' It was Gris

'Oh yeah she even had the CO's plastic cutlery off of him, it was a civvy 737, Danish wasn't it?'

Yeah remember the blond Stewardess?' Mike was articulating 2 hands over his chest exaggerating her breast size to help the story along.

'Oh yeah, definitely Danish, anyway when we got on board we had hot food, so guess what, yep 81 sets of metal cutlery, we could have really taken over the flight that day!'

Eventually the call came and everyone proceeded through the scanner, the Corporal was insistent that everyone put their watches in the trays, most people bleeped anyway due to their boot eyes and belt buckles , the guys had long since learnt not to be too cocky and just go through the motions, they could laugh about it later.

When the time came the RAF sergeant led them out to the pad, in front of the door was an old blue bus, the guys all loaded on, struggling to squeeze on with all their daysacs, webbing and helmets. The bus lurched forward and drove for about 45 seconds to the back of the aircraft sitting 30 metres away from the terminal building. Everyone looked at each other heads shaking.

They all bustled off of the bus again and were led in through the aircrafts port side door situated in front of the wings and the 3 bladed propeller, there were 3 metal steps that led up and inside the aircraft, to the left was the cockpit, Mike glanced in and could see the pilots going through the pre flight checks.

There was what looked like a full load of passengers, so it took some time to fill up from the back and ensure everyone was squeezed in. The inside of the Hercules was cramped; there were orange canvas seats down both sides, facing in. Then down the centre was another 2 rows, back to back, all suspended by green webbing straps from aluminium tubing. The seats were so close that when sat down knees almost touched.

They Marines were all sat together in the back of the aircraft, every one of Mikes group had flown in the C130 Hercules more times than they could count, Africa, America, Norway, Northern Ireland it was always the same, it was a bumpy jerky ride, the loud engine noise and the small square orange mesh canvas seats that would make your arse go numb after the first 30 minutes.

The loadmaster was a tall skinny RAF Sergeant who moved up and down the plane, stepping across the few empty seats, or between open legs trying not to tread on any of the passengers. He reached the tail of the aircraft where everyone's equipment was stacked on pallets with large nets strung over the top to hold it all in place, operating a switch the aircrafts rear ramp was raised making a whining noise until it locked into place, slicing through the streams of light coming from outside until it was cut out.

After passing down a paper airsick bag containing yellow foam ear protectors, he stood himself up on some boxes so he could be seen by all his passengers and, just like the steward on an airbus, but with slightly less panache and not as many smiles but just a little more enthusiasm he gave the safety brief, 'in-case of a landing on water your life jackets are above and behind your heads, the escape hatches are in the roof, straight up the yellow ladders', the ladders were their but the yellow tape that had once marked them out clearly was not obvious to everyone, just up from Mike and sat opposite was Sven. Mike looked over but he was looking elsewhere. Sat next to him was a slim blond female medic, it was quite clearly her first flight in a 'Herc' and probably her first time heading into a combat zone, she was looking in desperation for the ladders, Sven was never one to miss out on flirting with a pretty young girl. he was watching her as she nervously looked past him down the aircraft, and ever the gallant knight elbowed her and pointed to the middle of the aircraft, she mouthed 'Oh yes' nodded and thanked him, we all looked at him in that knowing way, everyone sure she still hadn't seen the ladders.

The brief over, and everyone settled back trying to get comfortable, squashed between his or her neighbour. The noise level increased as the throttles were engaged and the huge aircraft jolted forward and began to taxi towards the main runway. Mike's back was pushed into his seat as the plane turned to the left and came to a sharp halt. Obviously lining itself up for takeoff, it seemed like an age but then the engines began to roar.

The great beast lurched forward, all the passengers tensed and many gripped seat frames and equipment, trying unsuccessfully to stop themselves leaning heavily on to their neighbour as the momentum pushed them sideways, toward the rear of the aircraft.

Mike felt that butterfly feeling in his stomach as the wheels lifted clear of the ground and the aircraft pulled into a steep climb, the engines screaming to pull the laden beast up.

After a few minutes at the top of the climb the engine noise receded and the aircraft seemed to free fall for a second or two. Mike waited nervously and the aircraft levelled off, the white lights came on and a gloomy light filled the space.

The next thirty minutes or so Mike sat looking around him as the opposing forces of gravity tried to pull the huge aircraft back down to earth and the actions of the pilots tried to keep it in the air caused a series of sudden pitches and descents, like driving fast over a hump back bridge, enough to have the blond medic turn whiter than she already was.

After a while either the body and mind got used to it and ignored it, or the Pilots actually had control of the aircraft and things settled down. Everyone had the same aim, a little enforced horizontal time travel, in other words sleep! A few people moved over towards the cargo of boxes and baggage, spreading themselves out in various positions, they were the lucky ones, for everyone else it was the canvas seats, and 6 hours of 'numbness of the buttocks'. Mike placed his MP3 player headphones in his ears, then his large green ear defenders over the top, and as he had done many times before allowed Pink Floyd to serenade him to sleep.

After several hours of intermittent sleep the gangly loadmaster began to wake those at the ends of the rows, as they woke their neighbours Mike instinctively opened his eyes. The word was passed around to put on body armour and helmets, Mike looked around him it must be nearly time to land, it was struggle to find room to heave on the body armour but after a while everyone settled again, now wearing the bulky jackets they were crammed even tighter into their small seats. Mike looked up as the lights were switched to red and the complicated mess of pipes, valves and switches inside of the Hercules become less comprehensible. Mike looked around at the faces just distinguishable in the low red glow, all the lads have that buzz about them, this was one of those moments that made you feel different, on final approach into a hostile environment, not knowing exactly what to expect.

Mike began to think back to the first time he had landed in Northern Ireland, the smell of the aviation fuel, and the heat of the exhausts as he jumped into the soggy wet field. Then looking back over his shoulder shivering and seeing the green glow of the instruments on the pilots faces as the Lynx lifted off, and turned, then the abrupt silence. The helicopter had gone, and he was left with his colleagues in a muddy soaking wet field in South Armagh, he was just 18 and on his first 6 month operational tour.

He was of course a little older now and more experienced, no one amongst his team was under 21 and he could see and feel that the adrenaline and testosterone was definitely pumping. Sharing these experiences and feelings made the team feel stronger and would help to bond them.

He couldn't see the face of the young medic through the dim lighting but could imagine it would be in complete contrast to theirs, and to that end she was probably quite happy for the low red tactical lighting.

A loud whine signalled the pneumatics forcing the air brakes into place, and the obvious feeling of them dragging the aircraft back in speed, coupled with a reduction in engine revs, Mike realised the aircraft must be on final approach.

Then without warning the engines were fully alive again, revving wildly, something was happening, the rasping of the airbrakes relieved of their task, and the aircraft lurched into full life again. Mike could feel the pressure as he was forced down into his seat, something was seriously wrong, from the back of the aircraft a whistling noise could be heard and bright fire work like flashes appeared through the small window opposite, as flares and chaff were fired. The lights and noises could mean only one thing, the plane was being fired on.

The plane lolled and then jolted to the left, Mike was first thrown forwards in his belt, then held down by only his lap belt he was in the air, his stomach forced up toward his throat, no longer in contact with his seat as the huge aircraft began an uncontrolled decent toward the ground, a guarded fear could be seen on all the faces around him as the plane fell towards the earth. No one wanting to look like they were really shitting themselves in-case it was just one of those moments, but Mike sensed that it was far worse than that, they had been hit and were going down.

The passengers were once again thrown down into their seats, loud mechanical noises could be heard from all sides as the pilot fought the lumbering beast for control, he didn't seem to be having much effect, and not being able to see outside, and having no sensation of height, everyone was just waiting in fear for the plane to crash into the ground.

A large crashing and crunching noise came from outside as everyone was thrown firstly forward then more violently to the rear, lap belts strained as the giant aircraft lurched onto its left side, and hit the ground. The noise was thunderous as metal was ripped from the left wing and underbelly, sparks could be seen out of the small window on the opposite side from Mike as the engines were smashed and ripped apart by the hard ground. Everyone on board was once again thrown forward in his or her belts, the pressure on the waist was immense, as the Hercules hurtled almost sideways down the runway quite obviously out of control.

Just as suddenly as it all began the noise stopped and the aircraft came to a sharp halt, everyone had the same idea, time to get out, up at the front the doors were already opening. To Mikes right a couple of guys were busy opening the over wing doors, in the middle of all the chaos with the emergency lighting flickering on and off was the Blond medic, leaning over a young soldier who was sitting on the floor with blood pouring out of a wound on his forehead. She was busy dressing him with a neck scarf, Mike and Sven exchanged glances, in those two seconds she had earned their immediate respect. Sven leant down, 'come on love, we'll help you get him out'

The guys climbed out onto the wing with their casualty, lowering him down as delicately as possible but hastily as no one wanting to hang around on the wing longer than need be, it was probably full of fuel, lights could be seen racing up towards them. The load master was out on the tarmac shouting for everyone to get clear of the plane, the unique smell of aviation fuel was strong as the fuel from the wing tanks spilled across the runway.

Breakfast at Babs'

As they moved away Sven, Mike and the Medic looked back at the crippled hulk which now lay tilted over and lay settled on her left side, bits of the left hand wing, engines and other twisted fragments of metal lined the runway behind them. The medic broke the silence and for the first time they heard her soft Irish voice 'fuck me that was lucky'!

Chapter 4
Battle Prep

The camp was built on an old airfield just outside Basrah, it was a huge complex, a labyrinth of many smaller camps.

The first thing Mike and the lads noticed were the ships containers, there were thousands upon thousands, many were used to make up the perimeters of different parts of camps, and some areas were filled with them.

A variety of colours, age and condition they had gradually, multiplied up over the last year since the war. Many were now empty, some full of new equipment, tents, clothing etc, but all were worth exploring. With a burning and excited curiosity the lads opened container after container, they found everything from prefab bunkers, to generators, and paint. Sven was at one of the shabbier looking containers trying desperately to free the handle, Col stepped up behind him, 'come on mate, it's not worth the effort, there's plenty more'

'Yeah but there's something about this one, its calling to me'

Col grabbed the handle, 'yeah right mate, full of Stella and Heineken is this one!

The handle gave and the door fell open, there was a metallic jangling noise as hundreds of thousands of small silver coins fell from the container.

'Fuck me, you were right, hey guys look what Sven Blackbeard, the Pirate of Arabia has found....were rich!'

Iraqi coins covered the floor, and inside the container were hundreds of large brown canvas bags containing thousands more.

The coins were mixed but the majority were small and silver, just like thin 50 pence pieces. The coins were octagonal with a palm leaf on one side and a bust of Saddam on the other. With great excitement at opening this treasure chest, everyone climbed in and around the container, grabbing the defunct currency in big hand falls and throwing it in the air like the Great Train Robbers, it was all good fun.

Ginge was sat on a pile of loot letting coins slip through his fingers 'Hey I've got the film for tonight, Kelly's Heroes, Mike your Kelly, and Sven your Oddball!'

'Me...Oddball? you more like, you're the Ginger Gopper!'

With pockets jangling with a few odd coins the guys left the rest of the small fortune behind and walked on again a bit like kids exploring their new surroundings. In the centre of the camp stood two large concrete pyramids the strange shaped constructions were the roofs of underground command bunkers. Constructed from large slabs of smooth, grey concrete, and standing about the height of a 2 story house. The steep sides were just asking to be conquered.

Everyone raced up to be first, Marco and Gris almost fell off backwards but somehow grabbed at each other and regained their balance, once at the top Marco placed his digital camera on the top of the ventilation box and the group posed precariously near the edge. The picture taken, the guys skidded, slipped, and fell their way back down.

The next day started at 0545, as part of the acclimatisation process they would have to conduct a group walk, each day this would get longer, and eventually they would be allowed to run. However time was never going to be on their side and the guys were going to need to get used to the conditions fast. Mike had told them to try and work through the day as normally as possible. Unloading stores, putting the craft together and moving engines around in the scorching heat of the day proved how sometimes these things shouldn't be rushed, but there was really no choice everything was always a race against the clock.

The third night was spent in the tent listening to music and playing cards; often Poker with the liberated coins as chips, the other favourite card game at the moment was shithead. Shithead was an over complicated version of Gin a game of great skill and tenacity, whoever was last out and lost the game was taunted with great enthusiasm and delight by the other players shouting at the loser 'shithead', it passed the time.

It was about 1030 when everyone was bored with the game, and time to start having the usual discussions about Mikes favourite band Pink Floyd, as the opening keys of Wish You Were Here were playing in the background, Mike and Gris began swapping the same old useless facts that they normally saved to bore people in the pub with. Mike started 'did I tell you I had tickets for the London gig when the stands collapsed but I got called out to Kuwait and missed it', yes they all knew.

Ginge got up off his cot, and reached up fingers out stretched towards the roof of the tent, Marco was laid reading his book and looked up, directly into Ginge's off white boxers, 'fuckin hell Ginge you Ginger Gopper, put them 'stunt pants' away'

Everyone looked and there was a chorus of 'Urrhhh' Sven called out 'hey daywalker, put that ginger body away,'

'Your all just jealous cause I get all the chicks, they all love a bit of Ginger in them'

With that Ginge put on his towel and flip flops and walked out into the night.

Just as David Gilmore was on his second solo there was a sharp whiz followed by a huge explosion which made the tent flex, 'what the fuck' then a large apparition came storming through the tent flaps, momentarily tangled in the canvas everyone watched, then just as he got free again he fell across the floor, scrambling up Ginge shouted what should have now been obvious to everyone 'Fuck me they're dropping bombs on us' and jumped straight over his cot and scrabbled for his helmet.

Following his lead the beds were now empty and everyone was taking cover under the canvas cot beds, grabbing at body armour and helmets, most guys only had shorts on, Mike was naked 'they weren't mortars, Rockets more like, got to be' just then there were 2 more explosions in quick succession, this time not so loud, and then followed silence. Sven looked across at Mike 'shit those first 2 were close'

Mike was laying on the floor pulling on his combat trousers, 'yeah can't have been more than a few hundred meters away, not good, and look at us hiding under fuckin camp beds!'

Everyone laughed that nervous laugh relieved that it hadn't been any closer.

'Yeah, bullet proof canvas, I was more scared of that Ginger fucker landing on me naked!'

'Fuck off, I may be a Matloe but at least I know a rocket when I hear one'

Mike jumped in, 'rocket, Jack?' matloe and Jack were nicknames for Navy personnel, 'you said we were being bombed, did you think we were getting dive bombed by Stuka's'

The laughter died away as a head torch came through the flap, at the door way it was the company Sergeant Major 'your guys having an illegal party again Mike?

'No mate, Jack here though we were going to use Ack Ack to shoot down the Stuka's'

'No wonder we lost the Empire. You lot are obviously OK, you may need to go and cheer the nurses up later, they nearly hit the hospital this time'

'Shit, I'm sure we can oblige, give them something to laugh about, well show them Ginge in his boxers!'

The light nodded a laugh, 'Well were all clear now, we think it was Chinese 122 rockets, they use the big red light on the radio mast as an aiming point. Tried the same the last 2 Thursdays, but their aims getting better every week, better hope your gone by next Thursday eh!' the flap shut and he was gone.

Sven was sitting on his cot, no longer using it as a bunker, 'Is he joking about the lights, must be?'

Gris was taking his helmet off and re adjusting his sleeping bag 'Na he's not, I've seen it, fuckin ridiculous, at least we won't get hit by low flying Stuka's'

Everyone looked around and began laughing again more with relief than anything, unshaken Pink Floyd had moved on to the Great Gig in the Sky.

The next morning had been already busy for Mike after the acclimatisation walk, he had had meetings with various people trying to organise the extra kit and weapons they would need. Mike found the lads in the galley tent, or cookhouse as the Army liked to call it, everyone was sat around two picnic bench type tables sipping, tea, coffee or water.

Mike sat down and flipped open his note book, 'OK guys I've arranged for us to pick up our ammo and gear, we have a couple of problems though, firstly the quartermaster shoved one of the new grenades under my nose and asked if we were all trained on them. Usual Army routine by the book, if I said no we wouldn't be able to draw any so I of course answered yes we were!

Sven looked up from his tea, 'I didn't even know there were any new grenades'

'Neither did I!' sniggered Mike 'but they can't be that different, they still have a pin and go bang, well just cuff it when we get them. That brings me on to another little white lie, I also said we needed 2 Minimi's' the Minimi was a lightweight machine gun, that had only gone on general issue recently, 'I told him we were all trained, but just out of date for our weapons test, I agreed that 2 guys will go along and shoot on the range tomorrow afternoon to pass the weapons test, so good effort...... Sven and Gaz!'

'Oh cheers mate, fuck I've only ever seen one on the shelf in the armoury!' this time Sven nearly spat out his tea.

'You'll be fine mate, it's only a gun, anyway I asked to borrow this so we could brush up, here you go'

Everyone laughed as Mike threw the thick green weapon training manual across the table.

'OK on with the rest of the week, we have to crack more acclimatisation, we don't have long to get used to the heat, day after tomorrow we are all going out to the range to practice our live firing vehicle drills, so that means we need to start dry drills tonight, before and after dusk, to that end I need Marco and Dizzy to pick up 2 Land Rovers from the transport department, well keep it simple the boat drivers also drive the wagons on convoy. I've booked them already so just go and see the Sergeant there, his names Russ, better call him 'Sarge' though, he'll probably like that.

He's expecting you at 1100, I will hold the keys to Marco's, as I have to go all over the camp for briefs and planning, the other one you guys can use as much as you want, and don't worry about petrol apparently there's a wealth of it out here, although don't forget that's not why we invaded!

'On Thursday we will move down to Umm Qasr Port, where we will conduct launch drills, rehearsals and test the boats and equipment, once I have a workable plan!'

'Gris you come with me and well go and see the int guys, and start working on the planning and I'll brief everyone again at 1830 after scran, OK any questions'

'Yes just one' it was Sven, probably something about the weapons training, Mike was expecting some sort of comeback, 'yes mate?'

'Yeah, just wondered, why is orange jam called marmalade?'

'Fuck off' the laughter rose around the table, and the conversations continued.

Early on the Thursday morning the convoy formed up on a make shift car park 20 meters from the main exit, Mikes Land Rover was at the front, Sven and Ginge were loading on some water bottles taken straight from the freezer they would stay nice and cool for a few hours. The sky was still dark but the sun would soon be up and you could already feel the cold night air being replaced by a warmer drier breeze, it was a strange feeling your body still felt cold, but your throat felt dry and parched.

Up the road trundled 2 large Military cargo trucks, over each was a large tarpaulin to camouflage the contents from any prying eyes. Underneath on special deployable pallets were the 6 black inflatable boats, 3 on each, all inflated and apart from fitting the engines were ready to go. If any of the locals saw the craft it wouldn't take long for the information to get about, and there were only so many places in Iraq you would want to go with this type of boat, so secrecy was a component that was key to Mikes plan.

That's why they would move by day today, and train only by night, if he could have got away without risking it he would, but only a fool would consider going into a job like this without making sure everything was 100% prepared and everyone was 100% focused.

Mike stepped out of his Land Rover, and walked backwards for a moment and talked in the general direction of the guys, 'just going to have a chat with the truck drivers, make sure they are happy'

He approached the first truck and using the wing mirror as a handhold he climbed up to the window, sat the other side of the driver was another soldier this one from the Black Watch. 'OK guys you happy with the plan and the route?'

'Yes Sarge' both the driver, and the security number couldn't have been more than 21 or 22 years old, 'OK guys, don't call me Sarge, its Sergeant or Mike, I prefer Mike OK?'

They both nodded, Mike continued, 'OK you got fresh batteries in your radio's?, they both nodded, 'we are on channel 7, I will give you a radio check in a mo, I will just call you truck one, and the one behind truck 2, I'm Mike and the wagon behind is Gris, he's my 2i/c, don't stop, don't leave the vehicle unless we say so, and well protect you, all clear?'

The young heads both nodded, 'OK Sarge'

'OK that will cost you a beer; we leave in 5 minutes'

Mike jumped down and moved back to brief the driver and soldier in the second wagon in the same manner.

When he was finished and had fined them both another two beers for calling him Sarge he made his way back to his own vehicle.

Ginge and Sven were ready, with their heads out of the top hatch of the armoured Land Rover, weapons ready, both were exchanging banter with Col and Jon, who were conducting top cover for Mike's wagon.

Mike strode over to Gris, 'you ready mate, we booked out'

'Yep all done, how are the truck crews?'

'Young, green and keen to impress!....was that us once?' Mike smiled, 'shall we do it?'

Mike climbed into the cab, and placed his weapon down between his legs, barrel down, so it was ready to go, as he felt to check for the reassuring feel of the pistol in his combat vest, looking at Marco he nodded, 'OK mate, lets get this show on the road'

Mikes vehicle moved up the convoy, and led them up to the gate. The gate itself was typical of this part of the world, and although now shabby and showing signs of battle, had once been a grand ornate eastern style archway. With huge swords craved in to the granite gateway. Now it was barricaded both side by huge concrete barriers, and the convoy had to negotiate a chicane designed to stop infiltration and the ever feared suicide bombers.

After the gate they drove down a long approach road, at the end the convoy eventually turned right and shook out on the open dual carriageway, it seemed that the only real danger of death was from the crazy Iraqi drivers. Vehicles would suddenly cross central reservations and go up the opposite carriageway into oncoming traffic just to get ahead of the convoy. Then just as the guys were getting used to all the erratic driving, Mike slowed the convoy down, ordering Gris's Land Rover up to the front, from behind to cover their exit that would lead them off of the metalled road and onto a dusty undulating track. Here they had to cross huge expanses of pipe lines that hand-railed the dual carriageway, the track rose over the top of them on sandy hump back mounds, looking down the pipe lines they seemed to go on forever, they didn't of course they pumped the all important oil from the oil fields to the refineries and back to the ships to deliver all over the world. These pipes, some only the size of house drainpipes were the reason they were here, and the back gold inside of course.

They turned south now to follow the pipes, every few kilometres along the lines men were working to repair damaged pipes, in some places they were using cranes and mechanical buckets to replace whole sections. Some of the damage was from the war, but most was from the nightly attacks by local insurgents. A few bullets aimed at the pipes in different locations every night were causing serious flow problems. The Army was trying to police the problem, but with thousands of miles of pipe line that snaked aimlessly, it was an almost impossible task.

In the distance they could see their destination, the sheds and dockyard cranes of Umm Quasar port were beginning to take shape through the heat haze that shimmered on the horizon.

They turned back off of the track and again onto a larger road, from the front passenger seat Mike and through the metal grill he watched a convoy approaching, led by an American Humvee the top gunner his face covered in a green scarf exchanged waves with Sven and Col who were conducting top cover on Mikes Land Rover. The convoy consisted of articulated trucks, which seemed to go on for miles, every now and then another Humvee would appear in between, the drivers and vehicles appeared to be from all over, some had little flags flying from the windows, or in some cases painted on to the cabs, Mike saw the colours of Pakistan, India, Kuwait, Iraq and many more that Mike didn't see. There must have been 30 – 40 trucks; they were all carrying containers, stores, supplies and equipment to keep the huge American force equipped and able to fight. There had been a story of a container full of American uniforms being stolen, that sort of thing was not a laughing matter in a war such as this.

They arrived at the old port, now being guarded by the Iraqi Navy, the guard was sat under a cafe umbrella on a plastic chair, he just waved them in, Mike waved as they drove down to the long jetty, the huge cranes now still, that had once been busy unloading cargo ships from all over the world.

The vehicles pulled up, and Mike took a moment to look out over the river and across to the other bank, he spoke to Sven as he jumped down from the back of the wagon, 'look at this place, unbelievable eh?'

'yep its almost sad!'

'Maybe less' Mike turned back to where the guys were starting to congregate, 'OK, take a break, grab some water, I'll just find the Matloe'

Mike found the Royal Naval Officer, a Lieutenant Commander who he had first called yesterday to organise the use of the base. He was on secondment with the Iraqi Navy helping then to rebuild and retrain their Naval Forces with a small team of British Navy and Royal Marines. Mike introduced himself and was shown the area which he could use, Mike thought it strange that the officer didn't even ask what they were going to do, he said good luck and left Mike alone at the Quay side.

Mike knew only too well the importance of a good rehearsal, just like performing a play everyone had to practice their parts, not only to make sure they knew what to do and to make sure it all worked in reality, but more importantly what to do when things went wrong.

The plan itself was very simple a mix of small parts that they had all done before, but they had to be melded together and developed to form the final play.

Mike knew the critical phase of this operation was going to be the insertion, it was too far to go by road and the chances of being compromised on the road or at the launch site were too great. Mike had studied all the satellite photos and the maps and because of the importance of water to the livelihood of the Marsh Arabs for their fishing, reed cultivation and livestock their villages and hamlets were built around all of the possible launch sites, and if they were seen then the whole thing would be a waste of time, so the only option left was insertion by helicopter, and that had thrown up its own complications.

It had been a few months since the guys had dispatched from a Chinook and unfortunately all the aircraft were busy and not available to train with before the operation, so Mike had the guys had rig up the boats as if they were going to be dropped. Except today instead of a helicopter they were going to utilise pieces of plywood to make a ramp on the jetty wall, and using some old round plastic containers that had once held anti tank rockets that Jon had found, they intended to launch the boats over the side from about 2 metres up.

The boats were now ready on the mock up, Mikes team were first and gathered around grabbing the edges of the plywood 'OK who's gonna make the helicopter noises?'

Both the craft hit the water with a large splash, and bobbed up.

'Ok lets go, go, go' on Mikes call the 2 coxswains jumped into the water next to the boats, the 2 crews, Mike included, ran in separate directions 10 metres down the jetty and jumped in, this would simulate the boats being blown away by the down wash of the helicopters twin rotors, and away from the guys.

Down the Jetty Gris and his two teams were watching, and waiting for their chance to practice their launch, which would happen about 7 km North East of the first drop.

Once all the craft were in the water Mike practiced the guys in some of the drills they may need, in particular actions under fire. They practiced stopping and boarding another craft, then returning fire from the boats, what to do when a boat broke down, or when someone fell overboard under fire. Finally they practiced being surprised and outgunned by a larger enemy boat.

This was done at dusk then again at night, until Mike was happy that they had done enough.

When they had finished they craned the boats and equipment back out and washed it all down with a fire hose then repacked the trucks ready for the morning.

It was about midnight when everyone finally settled down in an old classroom where they were going to spend the night, with only thin foam roll mats to protect them from the cold hard concrete floor.

The dark room was lit by beams of gloomy light from LED head torches, as guys rolled out sleeping bags, and prepared to settle down, the chatter was a low hum, and the air was also filled with the steam rising from wet clothes, soaked through not by the water, but by the sweat and condensation from working all night inside their coxswains suits.

Mike was sat up on top of his sleeping bag reading through his notes when a figure appeared at the door. It was the Naval officer, he stepped over the bodies heading to the corner where Mike was, 'OK chaps, everyone settled in comfortably, sorry that you are all crammed in here but we have a course on so the usual bunk spaces are full, successful night Sergeant?'

'Aye sir, this is fine, better that the Basrah Ritz and we got through everything we needed to do'

'Good, thought you might need a little warming up' from behind his back he pulled a bottle of Navy Rum 'fancy a tot'

'happy with that, mugs out guys'

Marco was first with his oval shaped metal mug, he sat on the end of Mikes sleeping bag with it held out eagerly, 'just like the old days eh!' Marco was referring to the daily tot of rum that was issued by the Royal Navy for hundreds of years, until it was finally stopped in the 1970's.

The officer popped the red topped cork and poured the dark liquor into the offered metal mug, 'I'm sure you weren't even born then, I joined the year before it was withdrawn, I remember a story about you lot, told to me my an old coxswain who had served on the 'Vanguard', our last battle ship, in those days when the barrel was opened and the Tot issued, the waste, no matter how much was left, would be thrown down the scuppers on deck so it would go overboard, sometimes this was a lot of Rum, well the Royal Marines band on board saw this going on and decided to reroute the scupper and had fashioned various lengths of copper pipe running to their own barrel in the mess deck, very Heath Robinson, anyway it went on for quite a while apparently', the officer poured a large measure into Mikes mug, 'the best part was it was the Royal Tour with the then Princes Elizabeth on board, just before her Father died, so they could have had you lot disbanded!

Marco stood up, 'what would the Queen or the Navy do without the Royal Marines'

The guys all laughed, as he rose his mug, 'The Royal Marines'

Everyone sung out 'The Royal Marines' and took a swig, not to be outdone, and now feeling a little more confident as he had another fellow sailor on the mess deck Ginge rose, 'The Royal Navy'

Everyone made a playful groan, and again sang out together 'The Royal Navy'

Finally Mike got up, 'Gentlemen, the Queen, God Bless Her'

This was a signal for everyone to finish their Tot in a final gulp, the voices hailed out with pride, 'The Queen' and the warming liquid was finished, some with a quince or a squint of the face at the overpowering taste of the strong Rum.

They had already been kicking up the dust for about an hour, and were now travelling east, and so as not to set patterns they were following a different route from the one they had taken the day before. All Mike could taste in his mouth was the dry fine particles of the ancient desert, and the after taste of Navy Rum from the night before.

He felt constantly parched for liquid and his back was aching from the hard classroom floor. Marco was driving and had to slow down to a crawl as they came up to some railway tracks crossing the road, 'bumps coming up' Mike warned over the personal radios, the guys above on top cover braced themselves, it was not the most comfortable job in the world trying to anticipating the ruts and turns in the road, and at the same time staying alert to everything going on around them. The workers in the dusty fields, or the engineers repairing bullet holes in oil pipes, and of course the dodgy driving habits of the locals.

With scarves or shamaghs wrapped tightly over their mouth and nose, and wearing goggles that would get covered in dust very quickly the guys were the eyes and ears of the convoy.

These armoured Land Rovers had been designed for the streets of Northern Ireland, and although pushed to the limits were still doing what was asked of them in this extreme environment, but they were extremely venerable.

Mike knew that having your head out of the top of a top heavy Land Rover was no easy task, and with the threat of rolling over on the bumpy tracks, or being hit by a roadside bomb or rocket propelled grenade was not the most enviable job in the world. But sitting in the front cab, with no air, and no room to move, and the responsibility of the convoy it men and equipment, Mike was a little jealous of the guys up in the dusty air.

Suddenly from the rear Land Rover Svens excited voice crackled over the head set, 'Fuck stop, STOP, NO don't stop, bastard, I'm off'.

Mike and Marco exchanged puzzled glances, then Sven again this time with urgency and heavily panting 'Fuck, guys, BOMB, drive on, drive through, go!', Marco pushed the accelerator down, and the Land Rover bumped and rolled over the dusty road for a minute or so'

Mike was on the radio to Col who was on top cover 'where's Sven, what's happening, can you cover him?'

Gris's voice broke in next, before Col could reply, he was driving the rear Land Rover and had seen Sven run out of the back doors, 'we got an IED, right side, that's far enough, stop here, that moron Sven's ran off on his own, we gotta stop'

'OK pull over' ordered Mike….. 'where's Sven?'

'He just ran off like a banshee' it was Col who was doing top cover with Sven on Mikes Land Rover he had also seen Sven dive out and watched him run off, he was now covering him with his Rifle.

Breakfast at Babs'

All the vehicles pulled to a stop dust was thrown up in clouds, everyone looked across the field and could see the tall figure of Sven striding across the sand and berms, in front by about 15 meters but with the gap slowly closing was a figure dressed in a flowing black dress, a black and white chequered shamag flying like a flag from the back of his head and flip flops, obviously running for his life, the radio became alive, 'go Sven', everyone was in fits of laughter at the sight of the chase.

Mike looked across at the lads, 'time to get serious guys, anyone know where the device is?, we need to stop anyone coming up the road', Mike looked down toward the rear vehicle, 'Gris just drive out and around a safe distance and set up a VCP back down the road stop anything that tries to come this way' a nod to Gris and a thumbs up in return the other Land Rover was remounted and taking a big circle around the suspect area and then back on the road about 200 meters further up with the vehicle parked across the road.

Mike had the 2 trucks pull up behind his Land Rover and got the drivers out with their gear to cover the rear.

Meanwhile Sven was making his way towards the leading wagon, over his shoulder a figure wrapped up in its own dark tatty robe, Mike watched as he approached, 'who' your friend?'

'Don't know yet but he ran like a fucking rabbit' Sven flung the figure down onto the hard packed sand, next to the Land rover and pulling his pistol from his webbing, the sound as he cocked it made the Iraqi lose control as his face twisted up and a pool of wet sand appeared by his shaking body.

'you fucker not so fuckin' funny now is it' Sven was gasping, and trying to recover his breathing.

It was time for Mike to calm things down a little, there was a lot of adrenaline pumping and the last thing anyone needed was a bloody corpse to explain away 'anyone got any cuffs?'

Sven pulled out a set of plastic restraints from his webbing and handed them to Mike.

'here Marco cuff him up so Sven can come back down to Earth' Mike pulled out his water bottle and handed it to Sven 'hey that was some tackle mate, you sure this is the guy, where's the device?'

'Yeah it was him alright, Jesus can he run'

Listen mate I've got to call this in what's up their?' Sven was still catching his breath but was also coming back to normal and knew he had to tell everyone the reason he had told them to drive through and had chased down the boy. Marco leaned down and pulled out a couple of white heavy duty cable ties and cuffed the boy with his hands across his stomach, and dragged him up into a sitting position against the front wheel of the 4 x 4, then put a small plastic bottle of water in his hands.

'OK I saw this kid hide as you guys went by, which drew my attention, then I saw a flash of metal behind the berm, he saw me look and then ran, I ran past at least 3 artillery shells all wired up, I was just praying they weren't on any kind of timer, he dropped some wire as he ran, obviously just setting it all up'

Marco was looking up towards the rough location of the device, 'it's on a slight bend look, and just after those rail tracks, probably getting ready for one of those big Yank convoys they'd have to slow down so as not to become too spread out as the Arctic's crossed the tracks'

There were a few cars approaching the temporary road block, the locals were not too happy as the lads tried to send them back around, the problem was compounded by a distinct lack of language skills on either side. Marco was having a little success with the use of the international hand signal for an explosion a mushroom cloud and shouting boom at the confused locals, eventually this articulation began to work and they turned around waving as they went.

After about an hour the bomb disposal team turned up, after a quick chat with Sven, and a look at the sketch he had drawn on the back of a cardboard box, they walked forward and over the berm, dressed in their heavy bomb disposal kit, helmets and visors, Mike and Sven watched.

Sven turned to Mike, 'Fuck that job, they must be sweating their tits off in all that clobber'

'They'll be even hotter if those fuckers go off!'

It was dark by the time they were on the road again, the prisoner had been dropped off with the Military Police, there was also a short tubby local policeman, who whilst Mike and Sven were busy giving short statements slapped the kid around the face and hurled what were obviously well chosen Arabic profanities at him. Once upon a time a meeting like this with the police would probably have meant a long torture and quick trip to a sandy grave.

With the wagons parked up, and weapons and kit cleaned it was definitely time for a beer, the pub was popular because it was light and cool, built just like a large modern pub at home, with wooden beams and pillars and a long wide bar, the only disadvantage is you were only allowed 2 beers every night, since the same policy was adopted at sea it was never seen as a real barrier to a group of Marines, there were always ways around even this barrier.

The first option was to sweet talk the bar staff but it was obvious that even a continuous assault of complements, smiles and flashing of white teeth was not going to get them over the ration problem. There was always a way, it might just take a day or two.

Jon and Sven walked in through the double doors and over to the rest of the lads already on their second game of 'Shit Head', the backs of the cards were covered with girls in bikinis, Sven sat down at the end of the wooden table 'hey Jon this is how they should build pubs on union street eh'.

'yeah its crackin,'

'no mate I mean with sandbags and tape on the windows!'

Everyone was fed up with the cards now, and most had drunk their 2 beers, Mike had lost 3 times in a row, David Bowie was playing Life on Mars over the speakers, Marco was stuffing the cards back into their box which was held together with black tape. He looked over at Sven 'what a day eh, I thought I was going to die of laughter watching you run across the friggin' desert'

Sven was leaning back about to finish off his last Stella, 'well mate you would have if your laughter had set off 4 primed 105 Shells!'

'No chance, if they were that unstable your size 14 flat feet would have blown them bad boys up as you jumped out the wagon' they all laughed again,

Sven leaned forward elbows onto the table, 'Hey I saw Shirley Temple today, he's out here escorting the Army General about, was in 42 for Tellic, you know him Marco eh?'

'Yeah a Driver, bit of a muscle bosun'

'Yeah Right, he told me a good story, when the unit got back from Iraq, the CO got the MBE, presented by her Majesty at the Palace, so after he has the usual parade, has all the lads in a half circle around him gives a little speech about how well they did etc, then holds up the medal and says, this is not just my medal , you have all earned it, you should consider it yours as well, so one of the guys in the front rank put his arm up, CO looks over, RSM growles from behind giving him the don't fuck up stare, CO says, yes Marine such and such?, Marine such and such says Sir I've got my sister's wedding this weekend, just wondered if I could borrow OUR Medal'

The laughter erupted once again, Sven was nearly in tears and only just able to finish telling the story, the banter was relentless and would normally have gone on for the rest of the night, but today had been long and tiring, and tomorrow was the last chance to get everything prepared for the task.

Breakfast at Babs'

The guys all left together and walked back down the dark runway, everyone was carrying a torch or a coloured chemical light stick, the night was so dark and this part of the old runway was both road and pavement, either side was lined by barbed wire and containers, all divided up into sections housing mini camps for each of the units working here, each one had a separate barrier with a sentry and a unit sign.

The traffic on the road was anything from pickups carrying civilian contractors to armoured vehicles and tanks, and it was never quiet.

They walked through under their own barrier, and headed for the tent, it wasn't long until everyone was lying under their mosquito nets and the snoring competition began.

The next morning everyone was up early, Mike had told the lads to spend the day ensuring everything was ready and good to go.

Mike and Gris walked across to the Operations room; the room was the only one in the old concrete building with a proper door, and a key pad type lock. It was obviously not originally from this building, it was a large thick ornamental door, with fine Arabic lattice work, but both its top and bottom had been roughly sawn to make it fit the concrete gap. The bottom gap was quite large. Mike could only assume that the door had been cut so that the existing hinges lined up with the gaps in the frames.

Once inside Mike looked around, on one wall was a map of teh whole country from Kuwait in the South to Turkey in the North, also bordering Saudi, Syria and Iran, it was no wonder that this country had been involved in so much conflict over the centuries.

The other three walls were covered with maps and Satellite photos of the operations area, and up in the North East corner was an area of blue, through which ran a thick red line, the Iraq, Iran border.

The Intelligence officer was a young gangly Black Watch Captain, he had been more than helpful to Mike, providing him with as much 'Int' as he and his team could gather. There was now a piece of ply on the wall, covered in pictures of fishing boats, satellite images of the marsh area's and a 'spot map' which had numbered pins, with a key showing known incidents that had occurred at that location, shootings, bombings, or smuggling. There were also pictures taken from a helicopter overpass that had happened nearly a year ago showing close ups of a few of the villages that dotted the rivers, or the few bridges that crossed the waterways.

'I did an Internet search for you, we have a list of different types of water craft you may see, mostly canoes and small flat bottomed affairs by the looks of it. Apparently you can also expect to see plenty of wildlife, especially turtles, foxes, and even water cobras, I don't think you want to meet any of those'.

'Bloody right I hate snakes'

Mike spent had most of the day working with various aerial reconnaissance photographs and maps trying to match up the scales and also add in the detail that was missing from the map. The maps were a few years old and the water area was only shown as plain blue with no detail, the recent photographs showed many islands and several new water courses, which were not on the map. Mike and Gris decided that this was because the map was from before the war, it showed a much drier land, one that had been drained by Saddam as he tried to force the non conformist Marsh Arabs from their homes. Now that the pumping stations were closed down, and the population had blocked off the huge drainage canals, the water was slowly refilling the area and returning it to the rich wetland it had been for thousands of years.

Mike was sat at a large square planning table, the maps and air photo's were spread across it, with marked photo copies, and pieces of paper.

As Mike sat looking at all the information on the table the door opened and in stepped a tall dark skinned man, in a light green shirt and light trousers, his round spectacles were sat on a large Arab nose.

'Asalam `Alaykum…..hello Mr Stuu..wart'

'Alaykum as-Salaam, Mansour, have you met Mike'

'No no, Mr Mike I am Mansour, I am interpreter here in Army'

Mike stood up and took the offered hand, 'pleased to meet you, have you ever been to the Marshes?' Mike indicated to the maps, if he was allowed into the Intelligence cell he was obviously trusted, and local knowledge was always the best type of intelligence.

'No I'am sorry, I have never been, you have boats yes, I hear it is very wet'

'OK no probs, yes we have boats, we always use them non of us can swim, how about you?'

Mansour laughed, 'me no of course not, but I think you must try and stay in your boats'

Mike had been surprised before at the Arab sense of humour, it was often very similar to the English 'we'll try, well talk again soon, excuse me I'm going out for some air' Mike stepped out of the room, and onto a small concrete porch 2 old red plastic school type chairs, faded by years in the sun, were just in the shade of the overhanging concrete roof Mike sat down and sipped some water from the hose of his camouflaged Camel Back, a water bladder that the guys could carry on their backs or in their kit.

He heard the door open and shut behind him and Mansour held the back of the other chair. 'Can I sit here with you?' Mike almost said 'looks like you already have' but didn't, instead he indicated to the empty chair, and sipped some more of the cool fluid. 'Have you ever read the holy Quran Mr Mike?'

'No but Im no expert on the bible either'

'Well I am a Muslim, and I pray 5 times a day, I believe in the one God, and I believe that the Prophet Mohammad, Peace be Upon Him, was the Holy Prophet, do you know who else we believe was a Holy Prophet? Mike shook his head. 'No? Joowsus was the also a Prophet!'

'OK, ah Jesus eh?, yes I've heard of him'

'Did you know that we also believe as the Joows in Joowsus'   'No I didn't know that, I know a little about Islam, you believe in Mary and Joseph and all that too?'

'Of course, and you know why Jesus was sent to the Jews' Mike realised already that ignorance was the best policy, 'No'

'No? Really?.....because they needed him, and he was sent by God to the Joows, this is a miracle!'

'Tell me Mr Mike, if a chicken lays an egg, and that egg hatches, what do you get?'

'A chick?'

'Of course this is natural you have a chicken that looks like its mother, if a mother goat and a father goat have a baby what do you have?

'A kid?' Mike was trying to lighten the conversation a little.

'Yes a kid, a baby goat, it is the exact resemblance of its parents, so the son of God was born to Mary before she was married, this is a miracle, and Joowsus is a man, he performs many miracles he is the first Prophet sent to the Joows by God, but he is not Gods son, he cannot be, and here is our difference with your Christians'

'OK, I think I understand?'

'Good, I ask you is God a man? No he is a God, Joosus was a man!'

Mike nodded, his tone disinterested 'yes a miracle'

'let me show you something that will make you surprised'

Mansour opened his note book and showed Mike a carefully written passage, Mike read it carefully, expecting an oral exam from Mansour on completion.

Breakfast at Babs'

Surely those who believe, and those who are Jews, and the Christians, and the Sabians, whoever believes in Allah (God) and the Last Day and does good, they shall have their reward from their Lord, and there is no fear from them, nor shall they grieve.

'You see that even in the Quran Allah acknowledges other religions, as long as you believe in God, and you are good to your fellows this is OK, you are a Christian Mr Mike?

Mike was watching as a patrol was forming up on the road, the guys checking weapons, the drivers looking around their vehicles and the commanders having a quick radio check before signing out.

He turned back to Mansour, 'well my friend I was christened, but I'm not a Christian, I'm a soldier'.

'But you must believe in something!?'

'Um I suppose....I wanted to be a Jedi when I was young, now I just believe in friends, sometimes love and defiantly luck'

'I feel sorry for you'

'Thanks but no need, I'm happy, I have everything I want, and you don't see me killing my neighbour eh?

'Real Muslims do not kill anyone, the Quran forbids it, they would not kill thousands of people with a plane, and these people are not my Muslims'

Mike had heard this many times no religion openly condones killing, and it was all the more reason not to trust in any faith bar his own, 'Listen mate I don't want to be funny but I have watched Catholics kill Protestants, Protestants kill Catholics, Muslims kill Muslims, Christians and Muslims kill each other, they have all been at it for thousands of years, and now everyone's just killing whoever gets in the way, they are all doing it for what is probably the same God, it's been going on ever since people stopped believing in the sun and moon, and in those days the moon people probably killed the sun people, and the Orange Sun people probably used to slaughter the Red Sun people, all I know is almost every time I draw my gun from the armoury and step on a plane it is because someone is using their God as an excuse to kill someone else with a slightly different God, its all fucked up mate, but I'aint gonna stop anyone believing what they wanna believe, I'll fight for you all, like every soldier before me, and I'll let you believe what you wanna believe, but unfortunately you guys are being fucked over by a few wankers who are twisting those ancient words to prop up a fight they were always going to have anyway.'

'OK, I do not ask that you change your faith, but I ask that you remember that really we all believe in the same thing…really, and we all need God'

'Yeah I know, listen if you want to make a small difference, then come and talk to my lads, tell them a little about your faith, make sure they know we are all people with a history, and family and a future eh, remind them that everyone out there, whatever their God, is someone's son or daughter, or mother or father, OK'

Mansour stood from the plastic chair, and Mike offered his hand, the Iraqi held it loosely but holding Mikes hand as if he was not going to let go, Mike had found this a little uncomfortable at first but had been led by the hand by before and learnt that this normal practice and showed a mutual respect.

'Thank you Mr Mike, I would be proud to do that for you, you are a good man, you and your British friends, we have had a bad years, we must make it good now for the Mothers and Sons of this country, now I must go and pray'

'OK Mansour, nice to meet you, we'll try eh?'

It was 5 that after noon that Mike eventually walked out of the Ops room, Gris had gone ahead, and he had stayed for another 30 minutes, alone in the bright room he had been busy checking and rechecking his plan, often staring at the maps and air photographs imagining himself down there amongst the reeds, and islands, with situations changing around him and the decisions he may have to make, he had to be sure he had everything was clear in his own mind, especially with so many lives at stake, including his own.

Outside the light was fading he almost tripped over a pile of bricks as his eyes adjusted from the bright lights inside. Outside the air was warm compared to the air-conditioned building.

The buildings here were obviously colonial, built by the British last time they had had some control in Iraq, erected in the 30's and abandoned to the Iraqi's in the 50's they were now just shells of their former glory, the sloping tin awnings were battered and holed, and many of the walls had been punctured by shells at some time over the last 20 years or so. Behind one wall Mike could see a Russian built T 54 tank. Just visible in the failing light its barrel protruding over the top and through some old rolls of barbed wire.

Mike jumped into the stripped down Land Rover and pulled away, heading between the buildings and back to the main camp.

The day had been long and tedious, setting up this kind of mission need more time, and the planning sessions were always a trial. Mike needed a lot of assets, helicopters, boats, fuel, access to a reserve force in case they got into trouble it was a process of small defeats, then small victories until hopefully you got what you wanted in the first place, there were always a few compromises, everyone thinks when you have such an important job to do you will get everything you need, Mike knew only too well that that was bollocks, he knew what he wanted and what he got were two completely different things, long gone were the days of the private escapades of the Second World War, when a good idea in the pub one night became a daring operation onto enemy soil from a fishing boat with a few sten guns and grenades the next.

The signs were good that whatever happened the task was on, tomorrow Mike had to brief the Brigade Commander, it sounded like he was on side already and just wanted to be sure in his own mind that no-one was going to make him look stupid, and loose him his OBE for him, 'no pressure then' thought Mike

As Mike pulled up and stepped down Gris was sat outside the tent on a cot bed, 'all good to go then?'

'Yeah thank fuck, let's hope the 'Brig' agrees tomorrow. I just want to get on with it now'

'Tell the lads to be in the Galley tent at 1900, and I'll give them a brief'

'OK mate'

The Army called it a cookhouse, and the Marines called it a galley, but it was really a field kitchen, laid out under camouflage nets to keep off the sun, were dozens of picnic benches. The lads were all waiting for the brief drinking coffee and chatting.

Mike walked in with Mansour by his side, 'hi guys, everyone OK?

Marco nodded, 'yeah, but Ginge stinks of foxes piss!'

Ginge looked across the table 'At least I aint got a big fuckin nose'

Mike sat on the edge of another table, facing everyone, 'OK guys a lot to tell you, this is Mansour, he's going to have a little chat with you in a mo'

Mike took a quick sip of coffee from his mug, 'when I was18, I was in four five, and about to go to South Armagh, bandit country, we'd heard all the stories from the older guys who had been over the water before, and in those days Northern Ireland was on the news every night, just like Iraq today'

'We used to train for 6 months before going, and we were all shitting our selves, I was in a section of all young lads, no older that 20 I suppose, except our corporal, Sam, a big lad, great guy, huge tash, and a great soldier, he'd been on 2 or 3 tours already.'

'He sat us all down one day on a grass bank, and asked us what we expected, I think I said something dumb about Irish fanatics and petrol bombs, or some shit.'

'He told us that we were soldiers, and that we were here because we probably couldn't be anywhere else, he then said that if we had been born on the other side of the peace line, we would still be soldiers, we may not have blown up innocent civilians, or murder off duty Policemen, but we would probably have picked up an AK47 and fought, because soldiering was already in our makeup'

'Remember this guys, we are Marines, and we are here for three reasons, the first is we're too dumb to be anywhere else, but luckily we are clever enough to be among the best fuckin soldiers in the world. The second is we all want medals to wear at weddings, and impress the birds.'

A small chuckle went around and a few nods.

'The third and most important reason is we are here for each other, to ensure that we all come out alive, because in 10 years no one will remember this shit, and even if it's on the Wreath that Her Majesty personally lays on the Cenotaph with her own hand you don't want to be a fuckin poppy!'

'OK that's my sermon on the bench over with, Mansour here wants to cheer you up with some religion' Mike watched as the lads listened, and he saw the faces, the Sons of Mothers, just like himself, and hoped he would bring them all back.

The Brigade Commander was not the typical senior Army officer Mike was expecting, slightly eccentric and quirky, but as sharp as a sword, drawing on a cigar he asked Mike to brief him on the plan. Mike talked through the whole plan, right from leaving the base, dropping the boats from the Chinooks by night into the lake, the diversion, setting up the observation position, all the way through to capture of the suspects and where and how they would be handed over to the Black Watch waiting at the shore rendezvous. He was careful not to give away the places in the plan where if things went wrong then they would be in serious shit, Mike finished and the Brigadier sat back in his chair, hand over his mouth and thought, Mike had seen looks like that before, fuck he's seen the holes and he'll can it.

'Well Sergeant' he leaned forward again still looking over the Satellite photos and maps, 'be honest with me, what are your real concerns, which bits worry you most'

'To be honest the backup sir, we haven't trained with anyone else, they don't know us and we don't know them, Army, RAF, who ever' Mike was trying to be honest, but still thought the risks were manageable, 'its a serious problem, were going out on a limb, any part could go wrong, and if it does well have to wait some time for support, especially on the water, we've got 4 emergency RV's one in each corner of the lake, at best the flight time is at least 20 minutes from the nearest base, and a good 90 minutes drive in day light, longer at night, were going to be alone for a long time if the shit hits the fan, and everyone around here keeps telling me how busy they are already'

'I understand, but I just can't give you any more, the elections are soaking up all my assets, we can't postpone, we either go or I'll have to turn off the whole Op, the latest intelligence is that the targets are on the move, can you do it?'

'Of course we can, were 100% ready Sir, what could possibly go wrong?'
Jolly good, I say let's go get them bastards, what do you say?'

'Aye Sir, let's get em'

The Brigadier stood up, and towering over Mike, 'Ah yes Sergeant Cole, has the Operations Officer shown you the very interesting book he found about the marsh lands from the 30's?'

'Not yet sir, does it mention any Real Ale Pubs?'

'Apparently not, but it does state that Sharks have been known to swim up the Tigris as far as Baghdad!'

'Well let's hope Saddam didn't have them fitted with laser beams'

Breakfast at Babs'

'Quite?' Mike had a small chuckle to himself; obviously Austin Power's wasn't big in the senior Officers Club.

The brigadier turned his attention to the Major from the Black Watch who would be supplying the ground troops, 'you happy with your part Clive?'

'Yes sir, but we can only supply 2 sections as you know we are tied up with the northern sector and the food convoys'

'I know, but do what you can, these guys may need you in a hurry'

The Major nodded in response, Mike was not convinced it was a very sincere kind of Nod.

He threw his smouldering cigar into a metal bin and stepped over to Mike and offered him a very firm hand, wished him good luck, nodded finally to the Major and marched out.

Mike hoped the final nod to the Major was one that said, 'don't let him down or I'll have your balls'

Mike had only met Major Holden once before, he had introduced Mike to the young Lieutenant whose platoon would be supporting his team. He was a brash man with few manners and who had looked down his nose at him. He reminded Mike of one of those Cavalry officers that pranced around horse guards in their Jodhpurs, and spurs ringing, and in the old days would have bought his commission or been given it by Daddy, then led his troops whether he had possessed any natural flare for command or not. Mike didn't care for people like that, and decided to make it as obvious as possible.

'I don't care for your plan at all' snorted the Major

'Well sir luckily your not coming, I admit we need some luck. The guys are very well trained and will pull it off one way or another, they're Marines. Its being so far out on a limb that I don't like, but its now or never, if the intelligence picture is as accurate as I keep getting told by your Int Staff, then we have to go now or miss our mark'

The Major huffed, clearly not really listening to Mike 'how is your new recruit, playing at Marines all day I hear'

The Major meant the very young and impressionable Lieutenant Drummond-Smith, he was just out of Sandhurst Military Academy and very wet behind the ears, Mike had invited him and one of his sections down to train with the lads one afternoon, he must have gone back to the mess bragging about what he had done, the lads had him crawling all over the desert, digging in sniper hides, marking helicopter landing sites, and doing contact and anti ambush drills, by the end of the day he was wet with sweat and exhausted, he had blood all over his shirt where he had tried to lay across a barbed wire fence and jumped too soon cutting both arms, but he got up and tried again, the lads were just having him on really and were all looking mischievously back at each other as they ran over his back, and across the wire, but by the end of the day he told them all he thought he should have joined the Marines.

'He's OK, just needs a good Sergeant to look after him, and Jock Murray seems like he's got him firmly under his wing, and his lads are good soldiers'

The platoon sergeant Murray was a large solid Scotsman with a good sense of humour, and more importantly a professional soldier who had a good relationship with his lads, Mike had made sure that they all went for a couple of beers together the night before last, the Jock had bought all his Corporals along, and a couple of his lads, all Mikes team had come, he had stressed to them how important it was to try to make a personal connection with the guys that might have to come to their rescue if things went wrong. They had to be able to put names to faces, to make things more personal.

The Major wasn't really comfortable talking to Mike, he probably knew that Royal Marines did things a little different and didn't stand on parade for anyone except the Queen, he obviously didn't like it. He walked to the door gave Mike a 'good luck' that had the 'you're going to need it' kind of edge to it, and walked out.

Mike cleared up the maps and photo's that he needed for his final brief to the lads, they already knew the outline plan, but he now had to go through in detail, and also wanted to make sure that the most important elements of the plan had sunken in, what to do when the shit hits the fan.

Orders had taken nearly two hours Mike had given everyone the brief, but they had the gone over everything again piece by piece, timings, routes, grid references, code words, radio frequencies, there were also plenty of questions and things to discuss. What weapons, where equipment would be stowed who would carry what.

When it was all over Mike went for a shower, when he came back in Gris was handing out small square pieces of white material, 'OK guys here's some silk, and some pens, draw yourselves an escape map and sew it into your shirts or trousers'

Marco laughed 'this should be good, I aint drawn anything since school, if I have to use it I'm more likely to end up in Iran'

'Yeah me too, but just make sure you get the important stuff, and leave off the emergency rendezvous', you'll just have to commit them to memory. Don't forget the maps are at least 5 years old and based on information that's even older, so if you want to use some artistic licence and make a few things up it probably won't matter'

'A few more machine gun positions and maybe a few less Elephants you mean?' everyone recognised the Black Adder reference Sven was quoting.

The guys grabbed a piece each and began to draw; laughing about each other's artistic attempts, but most amusement came from the various suggestions on where to hide the finished maps. The next morning was hectic, the guys had packed most of their equipment the night before, and now spent the morning organising the gear they would leave behind. Mike and Marco drove to the front gate to watch the heavy equipment and boats leave.

The equipment was being moved up by road to a camp further north so that flight times could be minimized, here he would also link up again with the Lieutenant and Jock Murray who were busy escorting the gear up the main road north, this was the main dual carriageway that linked Basrah with Baghdad and the North, it was a dangerous route ambushed and bombed on a daily basis.

Mike had found a better and hopefully safer way to move the guys up north, the Royal Engineers were operating fast Rigid Raiding Craft on the Tigris River, a night move at 30 knots up an ever changing River would be exhilarating and give the lads the right motivation, but also give everyone a final chance to ensure they were happy with their personal kit before deploying out on the water operationally, and for the first time since the Exercise before the Wedding.

The drive to the old Palace on the water front was about 30 minutes, and it was turning dusk as the team unloaded all their kit out the back of the Armoured Land Rovers, a Royal Engineers Sergeant approached Mike and with a soft Newcastle accent introduced himself as Neville, 'we just got to cover a few safety briefs an that, an I'll introduce you to Ozz who will be taking you guys up tonight'

'OK, you guys done this trip before right, you had any problems'

'Naw man, but a lot of rubbish in the river, just have to keep a good eye out'

The briefings were over quickly, the Raider was originally a Royal Marine craft and most of the guys had operated or instructed on them before.

When it was time to go the guys split themselves down to 2 or 3 per craft, Mike was on the lead craft with Marco and Col, with Ozzy behind the wheel, a likable Corporal who Mike had learnt had transferred from the Australian Army a few years previously.

Breakfast at Babs'

As they pulled out into the main channel everything was dark, in the distance were the lights of Basrah, and silhouetted along the banks the shapes of large fishing boats and Dows. The 140 horsepower engine revved up and the boat pushed itself up onto the plane, Mike checked his GPS they were skipping along through the night at 32 knots.

As they sped along the city was spread out on their left, large buildings, old hotels and restaurants, mostly just shells destroyed by neglect or bombs.

The buildings made way for docks, oil jetties, grain silo's etc, here huge Hulks were laying on their sides on both sides of the river, one jutted straight out into the river, unlike the rest it was white about 100 metres long and lying sadly on its side on the muddy bottom as they passed within 10 metres Ozzy shouted down, 'Saddams old yacht, shame eh!'

'I expect some fly boy Pilot got a medal for that!' Col shouted over the roar of the engine.

They drove through Basrah and out the other side, travelling under a motorway bridge, and passing through the other side and with no lights things became very dark, the moon was just glinting off of the surface of the water, and using their night vision equipment they were checking the banks of the river for anything suspicious and the water ahead for any obstructions.

Occasionally something would show up in the river, a semi submerged barge stuck in the mud, and timbers, or barrels floating gently with the stream.

The scenery changed as they sped up the channel, large fishing boats and buildings were replaced by canoes and mud huts, and occasionally a small village, there was not much life to be seen happening along the banks, everyone was inside eating and drinking sweet tea, or thick Arabic coffee.

After about 90 minutes continuous driving they were nearing their drop off point, here they were to be picked up by the Black Watch in Warrior Armoured Fighting Vehicles. As they approached a torch could be seen flashing at them, and through the NVG's the distinct shape of one of the Warriors could be seen, the coxswains pulled back on the throttles and turned towards the light landing the boats bows onto the bank.

The Black Watch Officer was very friendly and happy to be doing something a little out of the ordinary, he explained how he had thought about joining the Marines, Sven and Col smiled at each other.

OK guys get yourselves sorted, I'll have a chat with the Rupert' Rupert was a common and slightly derogatory slang for an officer.

The guys loaded their kit in the Warriors and helped the Engineers carry Jerry cans of petrol down to fuel the boats for the return journey.

Mike walked to the front of the Warrior it was a lot bigger than he remembered, and this one had angular bars, like square towel rails, welded all over the hull and turret. Mike held one, 'for the RPG's I take it?

The young officer was unfolding a map, over the sloping engine cover, 'yeah we had the space armour retro fitted out here, its just welded on by the lads'

'a bit dangerous that eh?' Said Mike

'What welding?' He picked up a couple of stones and placed them on the corners of the paper, Mike smiled the guy obviously had a good sense of humour.

'No, an officer with a map!'

The young Lieutenant smiled, 'I gave my Sergeant the night off, it's his Birthday'

'Fair one got to try it on your own one day I suppose' The officer just smiled again, and pulled a pencil out of his pocket to point with.

From the map Mike could see the area was pretty deserted, 'mostly barren desert and wasteland. shouldn't take more than 45 minutes, the camps here' he pointed to an area marked as an airfield, 'it's been quiet tonight, they rocketed the base last week and a patrol was RPG'd yesterday, and we lost a Land Rover the day before, so it's interesting times'

Mike was soon impressed as the young Captain talked through the route to the base location, and the actions on that the vehicles would go through in an emergency. To carry Mike and his lads as passengers he had had to leave half of his guys behind. So Mike was briefed on a debussing drill he would need to use if they had to fight

'OK Sergeant, if your happy and no questions then maybe you brief your guys'

Mike nodded 'no worries, too shy Sir, its OK I understand'

When the fuelling was complete and the lads had wished their respective Raider coxswains good luck there was a few minutes for Mike to brief the guys on the Drills.

The guys climbed carefully into the back of the Warriors, it was the first experience for most of the lads. The seats were small and there was no room to move, as the heavy hydraulic door closed everything went black.

Mike had been in the back during cross training with the Devon and Dorset's on Salisbury Plain, He remembered it well the smell of diesel the disorientation and rolling that made you feel sea sick. Being tossed around and thrown against each other, or worse still into some unseen steel frame or radio fixture as the vehicle lurched roughly and screamed through the gears.

He had hated it then, and knew that this ride would be no different, and probably much worse and a little under 45 minutes too long.

The engine roared into life and the sound in the back was deafening, the 25 Tonne beast lurched forward and Mike banged his head on his rifle, 'Fuck' no one heard.

Mike sensed the driver was giving it his all, the Warrior was flying up and down slopes, Mikes arms were straining in all directions trying to stop himself from being thrown around and onto the other guys. Everyone was relieved when everything settled down and they were obviously on a tarmac road. Then Mike realised that they were probably now in more danger than before, the biggest threat to these armoured monsters was an IED under the road, Mike hated being crammed in here, and hoped it wasn't going to be his coffin.

Eventually after what seemed like hours the vehicle halted with a jerk, throwing the guys forward then back. Mike was twisted as it turned on its tracks and then sensed the change in sound as it reversed a little. There was a clunk of metal disengaging, and a wining noise, as all too slowly for everyone inside the hydraulic door swung open. Mike looked across at Marco, and said what everyone was thinking, 'fuck being Mechanized Infantry'

Chapter 5
The Long Road to Martyrdom

The white mini bus drove carefully through and over the winding and heavily rutted stone road that was the Gherha Pass high in the Zagros Mountains, which snaked down the western edge of Iran. The rugged terrain, harsh environment and loose stones made it a perilous road for all but the most rugged of vehicles; it was not the best route available for the old minibus. Their final destination was far below in the marshes of the border region, but after the ambush in Arak It was probably the safest route available.

They also had an escort, the two white Mercedes, were accompanying them to their next rendezvous. The occupants of which were all dressed in black robes, their AK 47 s held on their laps and under their dress pistols, spare magazines and knives, these were the 'Galine' an ancient Persian order devote and extreme in their protection of all Holy endeavours. Their order was more than 2000 years old, and had been formed from the Princes of tribes loyal to the Persian King and conceived to protected the Holy artefacts from captured or destruction by Alexander the Great and his all conquering army. Living by ancient decrees their strict devotion and ruthless manner had gone almost unchanged through the centuries. The automatic weapons mobile phones, and GPS equipped Mercedes their only real link with the modern world.

The convoy had travelled all day through the mountains, the children had been talking and playing in the bus, earlier the bus had turned sharply up a small dusty track that wound its way higher up into the mountains, after climbing for nearly an hour the convoy stopped outside an ancient building. The corners of which were rounded, hundreds of years standing alone against the high winds that cut across the peaks at this high altitude had smoothed the stone. Here a white Toyota High-Lux was waiting, 3 more children carrying leather school satchels appeared from the crew cab and nervously walked across to join the bus.

The journey continued the teacher sat in the front and would occasionally turn and in a strict tone ask them an important question or to recite a phrases from the Holy Book of which each had a copy of under their robes.

The teacher was not used to having children around him, and they often annoyed him with their petty demands, he did not wish to stop their fun on this occasion, it would almost certainly be their last chance to act as children. As of tonight they would not be allowed to talk, or communicate with one another again, the fore knowledge of this gave him a little sympathy for those young soles that he would help to deliver to Paradise.

As they entered the village the sun was disappearing over the jagged rocks that lined the valley, the shadow cantering across the ground, behind it darkness closed in almost immediately, the bus pulled up outside a large stone building, brass lamps green with age ordained either side of the entrance, their oil burning dimly.

The Teacher left them waiting as he disappeared into the building, the children were nervous, they did not know what was going to happen next, and waited in dread. After what seemed like an age he re-appeared, standing by the bus he now wore long black cotton Kaftans embroidered with golden needle work on the arms, and a large decorated belt. To the children he looked like a Prophet from the Holy Book, and at the same time the seriousness of his dress and look frightened them.

He beckoned to them without saying a word, as they stepped out into the cooling air one at a time, fear compelled Nadirah to stay in her seat, not wanting to leave the comparative safety of the bus.

All that they had been told was that this would be their final blessing, they had received instructions on how it would proceed. If they did not go through the procedure correctly, and with solemn dignity with The One True God in their hearts then their Martyrdom would be in vain, and on their sacrifice they would be turned away to reside with Satan forever.

Their teacher did not have to shout at Faiza to leave the bus, one look into his eyes told her that she should abbey and join the rest.

He now stood them in a straight line, in order of age. At the front stood Khalid, he and his younger Sister Nadirah were from a poor farming family in Tekrit, where Saddam Hussein had been born and eventually re-captured after his escape, at 17 he was the oldest, tall strong and arrogant, he was the only one that the Teacher had become comfortable with, he had renamed him Abd Al- Muntaqim, servant to The Avenger. If he was not destined to become a Martyr at such an early age he would have made a good Holy Soldier in the Militia.

At 13 Nadirah was the youngest of the group, she had moved with her family to Baghdad, her eldest Brother had helped move her, Khalid and their family to the city where the Americans were freeing their people. By the second month as the peace never came and the unrest became worse they had all packed up to leave. The family were staying with friends when their house was hit by a rocket from a helicopter, she and Khaild were the only ones to survive. An Uncle had taken them in, but he already had 4 hungry mouths to feed, but they were all boys and so would soon be able to work for their meals.

She was very slight and shorter than all the rest, and very rarely spoke. When the others played she would sit to one side and read the small tatty leather bound Koran that had been a gift from her Mother. It was nearly a year since Khalid had told her to pack their things and had taken her back to Tikrit, leaving her Uncle behind, but things there were hardly better.

One day soon after arriving back her brother had returned from the Mosque, and told her to pack again. They were picked up the next morning by a car and left once again, this time on a journey that would eventually see their Martyrdom, and revenge for the deaths of their family.

In the centre of the line and shaking uncontrollably from both the cold mountain air, and her nerves was Faiza, her young pretty face now covered by her silk veil. She had been 13 when she had left England, that was over a year ago now, she had been sent away by her Mother and Father who had deplored the War in the Middle East. They had protested in the streets with others from their Mosque, but their cries had fallen on deaf ears. Her parents had said that she should go and learn the ways of her people so that their traditions would not be lost forever, she was to be schooled in the traditional way in Iran, and eventually would return to Marry a good Muslim.

Her Father was a devout religious man who would one day become a prayer leader in the Mosque, and she was to be the perfect Wife after a traditional education. She knew however now that this was not going to be possible, and she had found another way to make her family proud. They had once been embarrassed by her leanings away from the teachings of the Koran, and her questioning, and complacent attitude towards the teachings of The Prophet. That had all changed now, and her Family would be Blessed by her actions as a Martyr, and hear her new name Faiza, 'the

Victorious' she grew a further inch as she thought of her Mother and Fathers pride.

After several minutes stood quietly in line, the great oak doors swung gracefully open as if by the very hands of God, only the Teacher and Abd Al-Muntaqim could see inside the great hall. The walls flickered from the burning torches, fire baskets protruding inwards from the stone columns. At the end a figure stood awaiting them. From his side the familiar voice of the teacher spoke, softer than his usual sharp tongue or monotonous teachings, 'go boy, take them unto Gods will'

It was not a Mosque but a community hall; the walls were covered in thick carpets that glowed under the flickering orange light. He nervously led the juvenile procession forward, and looked only toward the silent figure at its centre. He began to notice moving shadows in his peripherals, the hall was crowded, more people than could have lived in the small village that the Hall occupied, he dared not look to either side, and concentrating on the figure ahead of him, he led on.

He stopped at the end of the hall, in front of a tall old man, dressed in the same robes as the teacher, here there were no torches but brass and guilt lanterns held aloft by long thin ornate branches, copper or brass leaves sparkling in the false light.

On the end wall was a flag, it was the flag of Iraq, Red, White and Black, with three green stars and the Ba'ath party motto penned by Saddam Hussein himself in Arabic script between the stars, Unity Freedom, Socialism.

The old man held up a mega-phone and led the blessing, one by one the children walked forward and stood under the flag, and a gun was pushed into their hands. The AK47 was a symbol of their struggle, but looked too big for most of the small hands. The words of vindication that they had spent days in the bus learning by heart would be seen by millions of brothers, sisters, and infidels across the World thanks to Al-Jazera, The BBC and CNN.

After the videos had been completed, the children were honoured by a huge feast, surrounded by men of obvious wisdom, and Holiness.

After the feast the hall emptied quickly, and the children were left to sleep under heavy woven blankets on large rugs. A fire was being kept in the large hearth, two old ladies fussed over them, brought them some goats milk, and then tender the fire as they all slept calmly and in some luxury.

After eating a breakfast of flat bread, feta and haloumi cheese prepared by the same two kind ladies, they were once again loaded into the bus, the streets were now full of people, many waved and cheered as they left, Nadirah noticed a women, dressed all in black, she reminded her of her mother, and although she was covered it was obvious to her that the woman was crying.

The road slowly began to lose height, the sun seemed to follow the bus down, but without ever touching it, when the sun eventually caught them the bus was entering a large market town, they turned onto the busy main street, on either side makeshift stalls were selling all types of wares.

Women were busy buying produce, vegetables, rice and fish that hung by size and type suspended by hooks through their gills on wooden spars. Other stalls had large metal domes, heated from beneath on top of which women were cooking large breads, everywhere men were sat on their haunches, eating, talking and smoking.

The smells wafted into the bus, Nadirah wept as she thought back to her daily chore of shopping with her mother. They would buy food from a market just like this one, food for her brothers. The market was always fun, she would often get tit bits from the elderly women who ran some of the stalls, all the different tastes. Sometimes for helping her mother she would get something sweet, a treat of which her brothers would have been envious.

Breakfast at Babs'

The bus left the noisy hubbub of the town and now descending steeply into a large ravine that followed the Karun River south then West until the land began to flatten out as the sun began to set through the windscreen. When the sun finally disappeared below the horizon the land had changed altogether, the mountains were far behind, they were now in a land of waterways, reeds, and marshes', driving along roads raised on levee's and interconnected by old wooden bridges.

Most of the children were now asleep, Nadirah was still awake, the moon was now full above them, so clear that she could see the patterns on its surface; the stars were out and almost filled the sky.

They chased the moon for another few hours Nadirah awoke with the thumping noise as the bus crossed a wooden bridge and entered a small village. From what she could see in the moonlight it was a very small village perhaps 15 or 20 dwellings, clustered around a small river.

The children were all very tired from the long journey and did not want to be moved. The teacher opened the door and they were herded into a small white building, a women stood by the door to a small dimly lit room she handed them blankets as they entered, 'this will be your home until you are called to do your duty'

Chapter 6
The Drop

The camp was more of an outpost, another small area of disused concrete and tarmac airfield that was surrounded by large sandy berms with sandbag guard towers on the corners with barbed wire perched across the tops as if it was growing wild like ivy, and here in this flat barren and isolated piece of desert, a sprawling village of tents had been pitched and become another 'corner of a foreign field'.

The Army lads here had had a bad time of it in the last few weeks, locally there was a big offensive on, Alamarah town was only a few Kilometres away and the Elections were coming so the insurgents, militias and local groupings were all fighting each other for attention, but as much as they fought between each other there was still a common enemy, and the British forces had bore the brunt of this resurgence in recent weeks.

Mike had been told that one of the local Militant leaders wanted a Warrior as a trophy, the buzz from the lads at the camp was that he was offering a $1000 bounty, nearly 3 years wages for destroying one of the armoured vehicles, this had caused leaders of other groups to start a bidding war, to be the first to capture one intact, or destroy one. A couple of drivers had already been seriously injured by onslaughts of RPG's and improvised road side bombs, they all knew that at this pace it would only be a matter of time.

The trucks had now arrived and the guys were busy unloading and preparing the kit, the 50 horse power engines needed 2 men to lift them, they were normally just painted black, but the guys had glued hessian, strips ripped from sand bags, over the covers to help improve the camouflage and hide the hard lines and edges. Each engine was named so that it could be matched to its boat and owner; Sven had started the trend by calling his Doris.

Once all the kit was ready it was all lined up on the helicopter pad and covered up with tarpaulins so that any of the local civilian workers that worked in the kitchens and cleaned the camp could not clearly see what was being prepared. On the pad sat one of the two CH47 Chinook helicopters, which would deliver the teams to their separate drop off points.

At lunch time the guys walked up to the 'Galley Tent' a pair of huge half circular tents, with large hoses linked to portable air-conditioning units that fed the tents with a constant and welcome flow of cool air.

Mike sat down on the end of the long table that the lads had populated, as they were eating a Padre came up to the opposite end of the table from where Mike was. He perched himself on the edge and engaged Marco and Jon in a quiet conversation, Mike tried to hear what was being said but the general background noise made it impossible, as he left the table he patted the 2 lads on the shoulder then looked around the group with a knowing smile and left.

'What the Fuck was that all that about' Mike shouted down the table towards the others.

Marco looked up the table, a cheeky grin on his face, 'he says he saw us on the pad with all our kit, black bags, ropes you know, he thinks were going in to rescue Pat Milton'

'What the God Botherer?', Patrick Milton was a Christian Aid worker who had been taken hostage in Baghdad two weeks before, his captors had just raised the stakes and threatened to kill him in the next 48 hours.

'What did you tell him?'

'I said we weren't into rescuing religious do-gooders unless they were rich, and that the only Gods work we did was to help the gorgeous female sinners of Plymouth release their pent up passion, I think he saw that as plausible denial from a good old fashioned 'Tommy' and that was what all the winking and patting on the shoulders was about'.

'He must have thought we were SBS?, well let's hope there are some real professionals trying to help Pat with his prayers'

After an appetising lunch the guys went back out to the pad and met up with the Royal Logistic Corps Air Dispatchers that would prepare the craft for them, Mikes boys would help get the craft loaded two to each Chinook, engines had all been tested and the boats sat on rollers so that they would be easy to launch.

The second aircraft wouldn't arrive until dusk, quite rightly the RAF didn't want 2 valuable choppers sat together on the pad, so the first helicopter would load and move to a cleared area in this case the camp football and rugby field, just big enough to take the 30 metre aircraft. The other CH47 would then come in and load. Mike understood the concerns, the Chinook was a big target, 2 destroyed together by a single homemade mortar would be an unforgivable waste, and with the fleet overstretched in Iraq and Afghanistan heads would definitely roll.

Mike was helping fit Marco's compass and GPS on to his zodiac when a young Army officer came across the helo pad. By the way he was walking it was obvious that he was coming to see Mike, it could only mean trouble, so Mike carried on as if he didn't see him.

The Officer approached Sven who was by the tailgate of the truck, his single rank pip showed he was a second lieutenant, obviously still very green and looked about 17. ' I'm looking for Sgt 'Mike' is he about'

'yea thought you might be, he's over there Sir', as the young Officer began to walk over to the small group fitting the last zodiac Sven called over 'Mike, there's some Cadets here want a boat ride' the whole group began to laugh,

The officer wasn't sure how to take it so he just strode on, Mike suddenly felt a little sorry for him, and knew the lads would bounce him all over the place, so he stood up, 'Aye Boss, I'm Sergeant Cole, what's up?

'Ah Sergeant eh Cole?, yes a message from the Ops room, Int reports things in the local area are heating up, there have been a couple of ambushes against the armoured patrols this afternoon, and they expected that there might be a Mortar threat against the base tonight'

Mike realised that was probably good news in a way as it would mean the Warriors would be out around the perimeter waiting for trouble, which would not go unnoticed by the locals who would have tea and go to bed early instead, hopefully giving Mike's boys a clean get away.

'OK thanks, are you heading back up?

'Yes I am'

'Good I'll come with you; I need to make sure anything your planning tonight doesn't leave us out on a limb'

As Mike walked away his mind thinking through the time line that lead up to the actual drop the lads carried on working. Personal kit was placed into black waterproof bags made of heavy duty rubber with watertight zips, it was then strapped into the boats along with weapons, night vision equipment and radio's, everything had to be tested, checked, batteries changed and secured to survive the drop from the helicopter into the water.

'The evening meal was spent exchanging nervous banter, Jon was at the fore 'I've written me will, if ought happens I've left Cath to you Mike, and my credit card bill'

Mike looked up 'let's hope they get me first then' he looked around the table, 'Okay how about anyone that gets wounded gets a crate of Stella in'

'Fair one' Sven was talking through mouthfuls of pasta 'and if its fatal, then your listed next of kin has to get it, an no cheap Polish Pilsner from the corner shop'

The laughter was nervous, but all agreed, talk was always cheap when nerves were running high.

It was 0100 when the lads walked out in separate directions to the 2 choppers, the smell of the Avcat, the aviation fuel, filled the air as the pilots began running the 2 engines through their start up routines, the loadmaster was stood by the ramp checking again that the load was secured.

Everyone moved up in to position and sat as close to the rear craft as possible.

The sound from the two great motors changed as the pilot increased the collective and the blades began to bight into the air, Mike felt a sudden feeling in his stomach as if he had driven too fast over a hump back bridge, and then with everyone pinned down in their seats the 12 tonne helicopter pulled itself into the air, and was flying forward in a steady climb. It rose high over the edge of the camp, Mike could see the dark shape of one of the sandbag Sanger's, as it silently watching out over the barbed wire perimeter fences and beyond, looking for any signs of attack or the tell tale flame of rocket or mortars aimed at the sleeping camp.

The aircraft banked away and began following a tarmac road, occasionally a car or truck would drive along one of the two carriageways. Mike watched a pickup truck, the back crammed with workers lit up by a following lorry. It had only one light still working, driving along blissfully unaware of the shadows flying above them. A mile or so further back and coming down the road the red white and blue flashing lights of an Iraqi Police service car. Mike watched wondering where it was racing too but then the Chinook banked sharply to the east and away over the desert, and everything on the ground was black.

After a few minutes of nothing he could see the burning stacks of the oil refineries flaring off, some were 5 or ten in a row the flames at least 20 metres high pushing up into the sky, the smoke was so dark and acrid that it formed a shadow darker than the night itself, and covered the sky.

The aircraft banked steeply to the left once again forcing everyone down into their seats, the helicopter levelled out and began to descend, now flying low level, the ride was not as smooth as the pilot had to fly the aircraft positively over the changing terrain. The Tigris appeared below, visible over the open rear ramp and only about 20 meters below, occasionally glinting like a long dark road snaking into the distance, they followed it North for a while, Mike imagined following the river nearly 2000 miles back to its source, travelling over Baghdad and North into Syria, at one point only about 100 miles or so from the Mediterranean, before reaching up to its source in Turkey. Looking at it now it didn't seem possible; the lands it crossed were as ancient as time itself and the river had flowed through a unique time in the history of the world.

Mike was brought out of his day dream as 2 dark objects appeared in the sky, catching up swiftly from behind. Flying low and fast, the water was disturbed as the formation was joined on either side by a lynx battle field helicopter. Both equipped with TOW anti tank missiles and door mounted machine guns, but more importantly stabilised thermal imaging cameras. They were there to give protection and early warning against fire from the ground that the slower less manoeuvrable Chinooks were venerable to.

Mike felt a twinge and smiled to himself, a smile of self gratification, it had been his plan to get some air support and here it was, just as he had planned it. The 2 Lynx would later have another important role, first to ensure his planned landing sites were clear, and then as part of a deception plan, using their engine noise to cover the main insertion.

The landscape was gradually changing again, the oil fires were distant dots of orange and red on the horizon, below now were large industrial buildings lining the river's edge.

More thick black acrid smoke billowed from the tall chimneys of the brick factories; the smell was awful even from the helicopter. Mike had heard that the people who worked in these factories often didn't make their 30th birthdays. Mike couldn't even imagine that, he'd have been dead at least 4 years already.

Mike took a slow glance around the inside of the cabin, most of the lads were dozing, or pretending too, preferring to be alone with their thoughts. He could pick out Svens bright blond hair in the dim light, sat next to the broad figure of Col. He and Col looked like two love birds on a park bench, asleep on each other's shoulders, in different circumstances he would have taken a photo to show the girls back home!

The aircraft had turned and was no longer following any distinguishing features, but it was obvious they were getting closer; the ground below was shimmering more often. The little moonlight was shining bright, and reflected back up through the marshes and reeds like thousands of small pools, and tiny puddles. Mikes Chinook was flying extremely low over the ground now, what were probably minute adjustments made by the pilots seemed more acute in the back, engine tone was constantly changing, and it often felt like small sharp versions of the turbulence you experienced in a passenger jet.

Without warning the engines suddenly roared, the cabin vibrated fiercely, everyone was forced violently down into their canvass seats. The aircraft struggled at an acute angle to gain height; everyone held their breath as they heard the whistling above as the rotors cut through the air as if in neutral and with no effect. As the rotors failed to bite the air, and as if at the top of a roller coaster the helicopter dropped, and fell over the top, stomachs floated and then the giant beast began to fall. Now weightless in their seats everyone knew something was going seriously wrong. Faces in the dim light could be read, Mike saw fear everywhere, and felt it trying to take over in himself. The nose was pointed down at the ground which could not be far away, and the engines were roaring above them, struggling to stop the plunging mass of aluminium.

The tail gunner had been sat on the tailgate and was only held by a belt and harness attached loosely to the inside of the aircraft. Still holding the butt of his machine gun he had been pinned to the floor, and then thrown against the roof, Mike had watched as his metal thermal mug that he had been drinking from moments before, tumbled in slow motion and disappeared into the night.

At last the nose levelled out, once again they were all forced into their seats as they heard the torque of the engines and rotors get a grip of the surrounding air, and arrest the manoeuvre just in time.

As the rotors finally gripped the air once again the tail gunner crashed to the floor. He looked shaken, his elbow and forehead were seeping blood and with a outtake of breath just sat down in shock. His head white as the blood rushed to his organs.

Mike nudged Gris who had also been watching the aircrewman's misfortunes, and with relief both had a private laugh at his expense. That was a moment that would become a good story for the pub, but that was for later, and the fact that the pilot was a women would only add to the jokes utility. After about another 10 minutes the aircrewman quite obviously recovered, looked at Mike and held up his open gloved hand, five minutes. The lads were busy waking each other up, taking out the little foam ear plugs and undoing lap belts and putting on life jackets. Mikes legs were shaking.

Then the adrenaline took over, pumping around the body, like a drug, moments like this were what kept you keen, the adrenaline rushing through the body was a high better than any drug, just as addictive, but you hoped less dangerous in the long run. The 2 Lynx were now carrying out a low sweep of the Drop Zones using their stabilized head mounted night sights, checking no one was in the area to observe the insertion. Then to add to the deception they would fly up the road that passed the nearest village to the lake, as if they were just being curious. The noise of the 2 helicopters would hopefully mask the low beat of the Chinooks rotors as they delivered their cargo on the other side of the lake.

Mike, Marco and Col moved themselves up to the rear boat, they would be first out, Mike would be first off the ramp, he always tried to lead by example, even when he was really bricking himself inside. The Lynx must have reported back all clear as the aircrew man held up 2 fingers, final approach, the Lynx would now be carrying out dummy landings on the roads a few Kilometres to the west to try and cover the noise of the CH47's, and hopefully divert everyone's attention.

The pitch of the rotors increased again as the huge bird used its power to flare up above the surface of the water. Mike could see the wave size ripples being radiated away by the force of the down draught, it was time. The aircrewman was leaning back over the ramp of the aircraft, holding his retaining strap in one hand and the press to talk button in the other as he gave height and attitude angles to the pilots. Mike was watching him intently, the aircrewman nodded to no one in particular, and then turned to Mike giving him a thumbs up.

Mike looked around and gave a final nod to each of the others and with a push the boat slid forwards and off of the ramp into the mass of spray below, just behind it Mike followed his left arm across his life jacket down to stop it chocking him when he hit the water. In his right hand the bow line from the boat. The whole evolution seemed to go in slow motion, the Chinook was flying slowly forward as the boat drifted down through the air, Mike following it down, and into the water.

The water was colder than he expected, Mike almost gasped in shock and then felt the soft bottom of the lake with his feet, he pushed off to swim back up through the peaceful water, when he arrived at the surface all hell was breaking loose. It was like being in a washing machine. The noise was deafening, droplets of water were being thrown in every direction, nowhere was safe, ears and nostrils were choked full of cold water. The down draught of the Chinook was horrendous, the boat was so light it was pushed rapidly away from the swimmers until after what seemed like an age the helicopter moved forward to drop the second craft, Mike was still holding on to the line, and pulled the boat towards him, using the rat lines on the side of the craft to pull him around to the stern. Here he used the engine to aid his climb over the back and stumbled and fell into the boat. Mike then leaned over the tube and helped first Marco and then Col on board, without a word Marco lowered the engine and with only one pull of the cord it started.

Mike looked over towards the Chinook, its second load now delivered it pulled away and within a minute all was quiet, except the low drone of the out board engine, and the low thud of the Chinook disappearing into the distance. Mike opened his waterproof bag and extracted his Night Vision goggles, through the green monocular he first checked that the other boat was OK, he could see they were still sorting themselves out. He then scanned the area around him to check all was safe, with the Chinook completely gone the night was suddenly very still. Nothing showed up on his night vision equipment, he turned back to Col who had his headphones on, as the other boat swung around to come along side, 'you got comms yet?'

'Gris is booming through, but nothing to Zero' Zero was the headquarters based back with the Black Watch, the satellite radio could be temperamental, Mike just hoped it wouldn't let them down at the crucial time.

'OK mate no surprises there, keep trying, everyone else OK?' Mike looked around at the darkened faces nodding back at him, everyone was relieved to be on the water again, 'what the fuck was that pilot up to'

Sven spoke in a hushed voice from the other boat 'It was Telegraph wires I saw the pole go past my window, she didn't see them till it was too late, I didn't think we were going to pull up again, bloody Women drivers'

Col lifted one of the earpieces of his headset off of his ear, 'OK got Zero'

'OK send Pettyjohn'. All the codeword's Mike had chosen for the operation were named after Royal Marines who had won the Victoria Cross, Britain's highest honour, awarded for Gallantry, and made from the barrels of two Russian guns captured during the Crimea War. Corporal Prettyjohn had won his in that very war, at the battle of Inkerman in1854, out of ammunition he had ordered his men to collect stones and throw them at the enemy, who hastily retreated under the hail of rocks. Mike hoped they would not need to be so brave!

'Prettyjohn' told HQ that all the craft were safely on the water and about to conduct phase 2 of the operation. Mike checked his GPS and then his compass, and signalled to move off and begin setting the trap.

Chapter 7
The Waiting Game

On the satellite photos that Mike had used to conduct his planning the Island had appeared a lot larger and definitely more solid. They had worked it out to be about 70 metres wide, not the best place to set up a covert observation position, but the only place with a good view of the target area. As they approached the boat stopped in the water, Mike looked around at Marco 'we aground?' he whispered.

Marco shook his head, 'don't think so' and leaned over the back of the boat, his hand reappearing with a large chunk of thin spaghetti like black weed, 'shit, OK guys paddles out' Marco locked up the engine, and indicated to the other boat to stop, Mike grabbed a paddle, as did Marco, and together they manoeuvred the boat slowly toward the beach. They nosed the boat gently on what should have been the sand that the colour pictures had shown, but was actually fallen reads, soggy and rotten, so much for their interpolation of the imagery, Mike hoped he had not got it all this wrong.

Every step was taken carefully, the floor was a carpet of fallen grasses, the older lengths were dark brown and rotten, and the newly fallen ones green and breaking and cracking under Mikes weight, this area of suspended plateau was only about 20 meters wide and 10 metres deep, beyond and where the group needed to go, was a wall of solid reed. They would have to cut a path, very quietly and carefully through the centre and out to the far side of the tiny island so they could observe the objective area. It would be a long night, and they had to be hidden before daylight or the game was up. They had been told in their initial briefing that during the day the lakes would come alive with fishermen and reed collectors. Low level light imagery had been also taken during the dark hours, and the pinpricks of light that were probably lanterns had shown that a lot of fishermen stayed out through the night, but luckily this was restricted mainly to the banks and today was Friday a day of rest.

Mike returned to the team and briefed them on the task ahead, Marco would stay with the craft for now, guard the rear and man the radio, everyone else would help set up the OP, and eventually hide the boats. Even using the secateurs and a small hand saw the path was cut at a painfully slow rate, it was taking so long that Mike sent Col and Jim back to start hiding the boats, if they didn't hurry the daylight would be upon them. Mike was worried, he guessed that the Fishermen would probably start early to avoid the mid-day sun, which would give them about another two hours, he left Sven cutting and went to check on the boats, one of the boats had been pushed into a hole cut in the reeds and with all the spare kit and engines now inside it had been well camouflaged, but would take at least 5 minutes to launch, the other craft was however still afloat and Col was waist deep in the water busy replanting living reeds, handed to him by Jim, around the stern. This would mean at least one boat was ready to go at a moment's notice if they had to get out quick during the day.

Breakfast at Babs'

Mike carefully walked back down the cut path, the island had no bottom and was made only of reeds, like a mini mangrove swamp, the guys were suspending the cut reeds along and over the thick roots that disappeared into the water, and so formed a path that now must have been nearing completion, Mike used his GPS to plot the distance from the boats to Sven still busy cutting, 'the lads have cammed out the boats, our boat is still afloat just in case, you OK?'

'No this is shit, my hands are blistered to fuck'

'Well I reckon you're near done, I make it 60 metres, and we worked out it was70, max'

Sven looked up 'well I hope your right, this is my wanking hand'

Mike was right, after another 10 minutes of cutting, the moon could be seen glinting off of the water through the last few reeds that would become their window onto the target area.

The guys split down into 2 teams, one party would stay near the start of the path where they could watch the 'back door' and cover the boats, the other 2 would be at the front and observing, they finished off the OP area. Flattening the floor, and set up the radio, they then screened the front observation area so that it was hopefully invisible from the outside.

About 20 minutes after settling in to their routine and just as Mike had predicted the small boats began to appear everywhere, there were several river entrances meandering through the reeds linking villages with the huge lakes. Here the local population were continuing a tradition and life style that had remained practically unchanged for centuries, whilst the rest of the country swayed to the will of Kings, Sheiks and Dictators; they earned their living catching fish or cutting reeds for the markets of Al-Amarah, Bagdad and Basrah.

The heat from the midday sun was somewhat quelled by the shadows of the reeds and the closeness of the cool water, by about 1030 its intensity on the water had driven the fishermen to seek shelter and lay low. Some could be seen on the bank of the lake opposite the OP, about 300 metres away there were several men lounging under a makeshift lean too made of reed. Mike watched as they cooked some of their catch on an open fire, after a few minutes another boat pulled up on the small area of reed decking, and when the owner stood up offering a large Turtle he was enthusiastically invited to join the small community.

The day dragged on, the 5 man team went through their routine, 30 minutes on the radio, then 30 minutes observing, then half an hour sleeping, half an hour on rear sentry, then another 30 minutes off, if you fell straight to sleep the half hour flew past, but if you laid awake trying to fall asleep you could guarantee nodding off in the last 5 minutes, it was always the way.

Mike was on watch when the sun began to sink over to his right, they had gone through the routine of checking all the night vision equipment, and changing batteries in all the radios, ready for the night routine. At the rear Col and the other lads would be reassembling and re-floating the second boat so it was ready to go again.

Mike saw the lake before him turn red as the sun completed its work for another day, as the darkness fell which was almost instantaneous a cloud began to rise all around, Mike and Marco looked at one another, then the cloud thickened, small flies darkened the air around them, they were filling Mikes nostrils, so he held his hands over his nose, they were in his eyes, burning them as he tried to blink them free, his eyes began to stream as the tear ducts opened to try to clear the invaders, then occasionally a sharp bite as the hoards swarmed around their heads. After 10 or 15 minutes, but it had felt like an hour, they disappeared and it was all over, Mike looked at Marco, the first time he had dared to open his mouth since the onslaught began, 'what the Fuck was that all about!'

Marco was still trying to clear his eyes, 'what a shit-hole, its worse than the midges in the Scottish Highlands'

Breakfast at Babs'

Mike had only 5 minutes left on watch, and Marco had just kicked Jim so he could take over from Mike, as Jim came up and leaned over Mikes shoulder the radio buzzed. Marco listened, nodded then replied '3 zero roger over', he glanced over at Mike, and held a thumb up.

Everyone was looking in, waiting in anticipation 'Roger confirm 'Finch' over' he looked at Mike and gave him a quick nod 'Roger, on task now, out'

Finch was the code word that the target had been confirmed to be on the move, Mike didn't know who else was watching them and was only told that there were other agencies involved, but non that he would see!

Mike wondered where the word had come from, as he got up and started to collect the observation kit from the front of the OP, 'Marco did the other group acknowledge the message?'

Marco nodded 'yeah, I heard Ginges drawl'

'Right Jimbo tell the guys were on, make sure we take everything......hey and no noise'

Mike carefully walked through to the rear area where everyone was silently sorting out their gear, ' OK guys, kit on, lets get loaded up, remember we don't show ourselves until we have a positive ID, formations as in orders, lets do it'

The guys were ready in a short few minutes the adrenaline was beginning to pump; the boats were dragged backwards and out of the reeds and once floating again, were loaded back up with everyone's kit. Last on was Col with the radio, handing the pack over to Mike across the bows, leaning on the front he gave a shove off and followed into the boat.

Once clear of the roots and weeds that lined the edge the coxswains pulled the cords that started the engines, because the night was so quiet the revving engines sounded deceptively loud.

Slowly at first, with the engines revving as quietly as possible the 2 craft moved back out from their place of hiding, spun around and manoeuvred out and around the reed island in-front of where they had spent the last 20 hours. Mike was leaning on the bows of the boat with the Thermal camera in his hands, then every once and a while doing a quick scan with his night vision goggles, he knew that Sven would be doing the same in the boat behind, but also checking their rear so that Mike could concentrate on what was happening ahead.

Mike was concentrating hard, worried he might miss something, the pressure was on, all the intelligence work by who knows who, MI5, MI6 , CIA all the planning since and all the effort of the Satellites and the yank Early warning planes the AWAC's, just for him to miss the target and fuck it all up.

Col was the first to hear it, even with one ear covered by the radio, he tapped Mike on the right shoulder and leaned over the other pointing directly ahead and said in a low whisper 'hey listen, engines......outboards'

Mike turned his ear to the direction indicated, opening his mouth slightly, a trick to improve hearing at night, yes there it was definitely the sound of at least one outboard, revving quietly, the sound a low throb at the moment, maybe still trying to navigate the reeds or going through the masses of weeds that had caused so many problems for them earlier. Still no heat signature on the thermal camera though, must still be quite deep in.

Mike signalled for Marco to put the engine in neutral, they were all straining to hear, he turned again to Marco crossing a hand across his throat, signalling for him to stop the engine, it sputtered once then died, the other craft was close by and seeing Mikes gestures did the same. An eerie silence enveloped the dark lake; all was still, just the noise of gentle lapping on the black hulls. Then a noise, definitely an engine, then another, this time a burst of high revs, probably an unintentional twist of a stiff throttle handle, just like their own outboards if not controlled correctly.

They all looked at each other, the game was definitely on, but what would happen next, no one was sure what would come out from the reeds, or when. They sat dead in the water, everyone listened intensely, holding their breaths so as not to miss a sound. Every now and then they heard the sound of an engine, rumbling across the water then the unmistakable sound of voices, they must be getting nearer the edge of the reed wall. The sound was carrying more clearly across the open water now, refracted by the smooth surface, it sounded ghostly, yet it was very real, and carried a yet unknown danger.

Mike estimated that they were about 500 metres from the reeds and the area where he expected the boat to appear. The distance should be just enough to give them a good chance of intercepting the target boat, and hopefully take them by surprise, there was of course Gris's team who were also waiting to the North. Mike had positioned them there to either help cut off or intercept the target if Mikes team failed, and provide an all important reserve.

There were still so many unknowns, maybe the boat was heavily armed or able to out manoeuvre the Marines inflatables. He was sure they would also use a good coxswain that would have the advantage of local knowledge, and may have driven across these lakes at night many times before. It was that lack of local knowledge that worried Mike maybe even more than being outgunned. If any of Mikes teams ran aground or hit any of the islands not plotted on the maps they would be sitting ducks, and an inflatable boat with only rubber and air walls was no place to defend from.

Mike could hear some more chatter, the voices clearer now, and the distinct low hum of an engine. Suddenly Mike got a thermal picture, the white heat of 2 men standing on a long black shape, at the back the glow of a very hot outboard were contrasted by the cold back background.

Mike pressed the pressel on his personal radio 'I have them, 1 O' clock of bows, 2 guys, long canoe, single engine, moving right to left' then using a flat hand, but still looking into his scope, he pointed in the direction of the boat.

Mikes heart was racing, he had to calm himself, it could be fishermen, and if he compromised the whole mission chasing a couple of fishermen he'd be a laughing stock, lads wouldn't be too impressed either after all the effort.

The others followed his hand and stared into the dark, the boat was still out of range for their NVG's, they could only listen, and watch for the team leaders signals.

Now clear of the reeds Mike expected the boat to begin its dash across the lake, instead it halted and sat on the edge of the reeds just slowly drifting across the front with the wind.

Mike waited for the fishing rods to appear.
The craft turned and reversed its track, something was wrong, maybe they were just being cautious, if they were that professional, or worried surely they would cut their engine and listen just as Mike was doing, maybe its not the target after all.

Just as Mike was about to press the pressel and tell the lads the bad news another boat appeared from the reeds, a slightly longer boat, the coxswain stood high on the back, again an engine glowing hot from working hard in the confined channel between the reeds, but this one was different, on the very front stood another man, he had something long by his side, Mike kept staring, hoping it was a rifle not a fishing rod. In between the two men, and much lower, were more heat signatures. Mike tried to make them out they were slightly smaller, but then one moved, sat in the bottom of the boat were several heads, it was hard to tell how many, perhaps 4 or 5.

'OK here's boat 2, coxswain on the stern, guy on the bow, holding something AK size, and about 5 passengers, sat on the floor'. The boat moved out onto the edge of the lake and again seemed to wait. There seemed to be no dash across the dark lake as Mike had been expecting, until from the reeds a third craft appeared.

Shit, there's three.

Mike remembered no one else could see yet, he pressed the pressel, 'Shit, there's 3' Mike whispered as well as giving the hand signal. He waiting for a while, the three craft closed together for a moment, perhaps talking about their next plan, and then drifted apart again, all now slowly moving away from the reeds.

Mike was sure this was it.

'Col send 'Haliday', they will be on the move any minute'

Col spoke quietly and clearly across the boom mike, 'All callsigns this is 3 Zero, Haliday 3, say again Haliday 3 over' the 3 added to the code word would let the other teams up North know they could expect 3 enemy craft.

Everyone was waiting in anticipation for Mike's next decision, the one that could mean success or failure. The key to any successful operation was surprise, in this case when to begin their pursuit, and in doing so show their hand to the enemy. Too soon and the surprise would be lost the enemy boats could split and run back to disappear once again in amongst the reeds, too late and they might not be able to catch their quarry at all.

Over by the edge of the lake they heard the unmistakable sound of outboard engines screaming to life as throttles opening up and the 3 craft began the dash that Mike had anticipated. Mike guessed they would want to stay on the open water of the lake for as little time as possible, they probably assumed their only threat at this time was being surprised by a Coalition helicopter.

As Mike watched, through the thermal imager it was clear that the 2 shorter craft with the security and had taken up station one in-front and one behind the larger craft carrying the passengers, as the picture grew in his scope and became clearer it was easy to see the long cold dark objects showing black against the hot bodies, everyone was carrying a weapon and it was ready to use.

Mike could talk to the guys now, the noise of the engines would deafen those on board the other craft 'OK guys there are 3 boats, the middle one is the target craft, we go straight for her, Sven you guys cover us but try to take out the rear boat as we close, and we'll hope that the front boat cant fire back very well, Gris and the others distract him as they close from the North, everyone set?'

Mike looked around everyone was nodding or givin the thumbs up, Marco was the only one to speak 'lets fuckin do it'

'Yeah, lets Fuckin do it, Col send Hunter South' engines were started in a flash, and everyone crouched down in the boat, weapons up ready in the shoulder, Col was on the radio, 'All call signs this is 3 zero, Hunter South'. This time the code word would not only let everyone know that they were in pursuit, but that Mike wanted the other group to close in a Southerly direction straight away instead of waiting in ambush to pounce. He had decided that they would need more firepower at the critical moment.

The boats were closing from slightly behind the enemy group, hoping not to be seen too soon, hopefully the guys driving the boats were concentrating on not running into the boat in front or an obstacle in the water instead of looking around, and the sounds of the engines screaming in their ears would mask the noise of the approaching back rubber boats.

They were now less than 200 meters away, just a little longer and they could show their hand, Mike was trying to use the night sight mounted on his rifle to help choose his moment but with the small boat bouncing all over the place it was almost impossible to get more than a couple of seconds of clear picture at a time. The metal scope almost knocked him out twice. However as the boat settled for a moment in the still between the wakes of the speeding craft Mike could briefly make out the middle boat quite clearly, the heads sat down the middle were definitely smaller than the rest, perhaps they were women, one of the heads rose, an arm reached toward the man at the front, touching him briefly, then quite clearly pointed straight at Mikes boat.

'Shit' no time to tell anyone, as he squeezed the trigger Mike shouted, 'They've seen us' cursing himself as he did, knowing the rounds were wasted, he switched aim to the man driving at the rear of the nearest boat, and let off 5 rounds, as all around him hell broke loose.

They were now closing on the rear boat, exchanging rounds to try to keep the pressure on, but knowing a direct hit would be pure luck at this range. Mike shouted at Sven and Jon to concentrate on the rear boat so he could switch fire on the middle boat. Col was engaging the man who was now kneeling in the bows of the rear boat and firing erratically toward Col and then at the rear Zodiac, the AK47 rounds just missing his own coxswain.

Mike was trying desperately to get some accurate shots off at the driver of the second boat. It was hard to take aim, they were now getting closer but the small inflatable was being thrown around by the wash of the enemy boats, and Mike was conscious of the small heads.

Marco's driving skills brought them up and in front of the rear boat and a quick glance behind he could see the red tracer as Sven was engaging it, rounds were also being returned and the fire fight was very intense, the bright red flashes now joined by the green tracer of the Kalashnikov rifles. Ahead the front boat was beginning to turn obviously intending to come around and assist the others. Then Mike heard a fizzing sound and a stream of light as high above white flares popped and lit up the night sky. Everything was now illuminated by burning yellowish lights fired by the Northern group who were closing fast but yet unsure how to help. The man in the front boat began to point at the approaching craft and shouted at his driver, the boat turned back North to try to fend off the new threat.

Mike shouted to no one in particular, 'good effort Gris, thank fuck'

It was time to concentrate on stopping this boat, Mike tried to use the black tube to support him, he shouted back at Marco 'keep her steady, Col get the driver' he fired 2 shots in quick succession, missed! Mike took aim again, 'Marco, steady' he fired again, this time the man driving was thrown backwards and twisted away off the back of the boat and into the black water,

Mike shouted out without thinking, 'take that fucker!' he hardly had time to regret his outburst when without its driver to control the engine the outboard swung suddenly over causing the boat to veer towards them.

Marco saw the sudden and violent movement that threw the sharp bows of the long boat into their path, throwing the occupants down into the bottom. Marco acted quickly trying to avoid the collision but it was too late, the 2 bows collided, the long wooden hull riding up and over the front of the inflatable, it drove directly at Col and with nowhere else to go he threw himself overboard, his radio headset still on his head, the lead parting from the radio with the force.

The wooden hull pierced the rubber skin at the same time, almost immediately deflating one of the front tubes and causing the 50 horse power engine to drive the Marines boat down under the other, and yet deeper under the water, before the remaining air pushed it back up, jamming the two craft together.

Mike found himself on his back under water, with the other wooden hull over him; he had to wriggle out using all his strength to get clear of the boat and water.

As Mike pulled himself clear he was still on his back in the bottom of the flooded inflatable.

Relieved to be free he was about to heave himself up when a foot was planted firmly on his chest, he looked up into the face of his enemy.

Standing above him in his chequered shirt and thick rimmed glasses was a tall man, with an angry determined expression.

His eyes ablaze, Mike could read the hatred and anger as he levelled the barrel of the Kalashnikov directly at Mikes head.

Mike was angry too, the adrenaline was pumping through him, he opened his mouth to speak just as 2 shots rang out in close succession. The noise made Mike heart stop, his eyes involuntarily closed tight, anticipating the burning agony, but there was no pain.

Mike forced his eyes open to see the man jerk backwards screaming as he did, his left hand clutching his shoulder, as he was thrown from the boat, and with a splash hit the water.

Marco practically fell into the boat next to Mike and gripped his mates shoulder in a firm grip, his Browning pistol held up in his other hand, 'you OK Mate.....that's a crate'

'Yeah...I'm OK, Fuck that was close, is Amstel OK?!' Mike sat up, 'what a Fuckin mess, Jesus, where the Fucks Col?'

'I'm here, thanks for your obvious concern!' Mike and Marco looked over the canoe to see Col, wet from his head down, headset still on his head climbing up and over the back of the boat, using the engine to pull himself clear of the water.

Marco smiled and looked at Mike 'that's a definitely a crate, leaving the boat without the coxswains permission!'

Mike smiled at Col who was now dripping in the flooded stern 'Fair one, right let's see what we have here. Cover me Marco'

Mike pulled up his rifle, quickly checked it, the safety was still off, Mike pointed to Col and gave him a thumbs up, Marco nodded, from a kneeling position both men rose rifle shouldered and pistol ready.

They both look down into the canoe, and there cowering down the centre were five children, three boys and towards the back and huddled together the unmistakable robes of two young girls. Their eyes were wide in panic, obviously shaken from the chase and the gun fire. Some were mumbling what Mike assumed must have been prayers, and although the night was warm most were shaking. Poor Bastards thought Mike, they were waiting to hear the guns again the spray of bullets that would finish them off..

Mike looked down the line again, there sat at the very front of the group and with his eyes burning with the same pure hate Mike had seen only minutes before in his teacher, was an older boy, his shoulders stiff, and his face like stone.

Marco tried one of the only Arabic phrases he was any good at remembering 'Salaam Alaikum'

The older boy began to shout back at Marco in course Arabic, he was pointing at their guns, and then at his siblings, as if he was willing Mike and Marco to shoot them all, 'peace be with you too mate'.

'Well that went fuckin well Marco, perhaps you should work for the UN, right, let's take this canoe back to shore, Col if you start transferring the kit over, then well slash the Zodiac and sink her'

'Marco see how the engine is maybe we can drive her in'

Mike looked around, it seems everyone else had fared a little better than his crew, the wooded boat that had been up front leading the group now had two rubber boats tied either side and it was being towed back towards the others with Sven standing in the bows like Nelson after the battle of the Nile.

Ginge came over and pleaded with Mike not to sink the boat with a brand new engine on, but there wasn't much room in the already over loaded boats. Sorry mate I know how much you love them all, but we aint got time to fuck about, and it's a big firm, the Queen will buy you a new one when we get home, OK?

'I suppose, just such a waste'

Mike this engine is fucked, the rounds have gone straight through the cylinder'

'Wasn't me I didn't hit fuck all', how about our outboard, will it fit Ginge?'

'No mate, waste of time the shafts too short'

'How about the other canoe?

Same as this one, you guys just don't like engines!'

Mike realised they had been a little keen he had told them in orders to shoot at the engines to stop the boats, it had been a mistake, 'Shit its going to be a long night'

'OK Ginge, you got you big knife we gave you?,

Ginge nodded and grabbed the long handled knife from his webbing.

'start slashing the Zodiac'

Sinking a rubber boat designed to float isn't easy, but Mike hoped the weight of the engine would help it go down, normally they would have fragged it with a grenade, but Mike didn't want any more noise or light than was necessary, so Ginge slashed each of the remaining 4 tubes, whilst Gaz leaned over from the other boat and removed all the valves.

Mike looked around him, they were exposed and had to go, one of the canoes had escaped, and it wouldn't take long for them to return and try to reclaim their obviously valuable cargo.

'Col send 'Finch' mate I'll brief everyone and then let's get going' The code word 'Finch would see the Chinook and the 2 Lynx airborne, and give the boats enough time to make it to the shore side rendezvous. Here the troops would be waiting to secure both the landing site for the boats and a couple of hundred metres away the one for the helicopter, Col was busy with the radio, the headset was now seemingly useless, and he was now talking into a handset that resembled an old 1980's trim phone, 'Hello Zero this is Golf Three One Radio Check Over'

Mike was now standing in Jims boat and had called the other 2 craft in to him, so he could brief everyone, he had heard Col call the radio check several times, 'Right guys seems we don't have comms no surprises there, were down to 3 craft, 2 will support front and rear, mine front, Sven rear and Jon you tow the Canoe, it'll be slow, just be ready for any of those fuckers coming back for us. Well head North to RV 1, if all goes wrong, land destroy the boats and make your way to the shore ERV and the Helo, don't forget we have 2 Lynx for support, make sure you make it obvious to them that your friendlies, any questions?' Mike looked around the faces, everyone was still alive, and alert, and he could tell by the looks, ready..... 'Right less go'

Jon and Dizzy were securing the canoe to a line on the back of the rubber boat, tied with a slip knot so they could release it quickly. There was no room for the children in the Zodiacs now that they only had 3 craft. Mike also wanted to be able to separate the canoe in case they ran into trouble; he didn't fancy the deaths of any kids on his conscience.

Towing the canoe would seriously slow them down, there was no time to waste. Mike knew that they had to get going, before more trouble found them.

Mike signalled for Jim to drive on, pointing with a flat hand into the dark ahead, Jim nodded pushed the engine leaver forward and increased the throttle, Mike looked at Col, 'any luck?'

Col shook his head, the canoe had driven over the Radio and snapped the antenna off, Col had used a piece of cable to improvise a replacement, but it wasn't working, 'the sat comms are shagged, our only chance is the direct comms with the helo or ground teams and then only when they get close enough'

'How close?' Mike dreaded the answer.

The tone of Cols voice indicated his frustration 'with this shit, close enough to shout should do it!'

Mike had told the Headquarters that if they had no comms after 30 minutes of the initial chase to put the aircraft in the air anyway. He had hoped to have seen at least one of the Lynx by now that would give over-watch to cover them and eventually the Chinook as it approached. As the 3 remaining craft started off in the direction of the RV, Mike was feeling anxious. Although things had gone reasonably well so far, they had lost a boat, and now had more passengers than he expected, and especially without communications Mikes gut feeling was things were only going to get worse, he was yet to realise how much worse.

Mike began to consider the Children they had surprised him, were they cover, or just passengers or maybe children of highly placed militia or fanatic leaders, maybe the security services wanted them as bargaining chips, as improbable and immoral as it first seemed the security services, MI5 and the CIA had their own way of doing things, and to them often the end result far outweighed how you got there.

Mike looked across at the edges of the lakes which were just becoming visible in the dark; from here it looked like an impregnable wall of thick marsh grass. Mike knew from careful study of the Satellite photo's that there were numerous small entrances leading to channels and tributaries. These then wound their way upstream to the small villages and hamlets that had grown up around the lakes. The villages themselves were congregated around where these waterways were fed by the long straight canals that irrigated across the farmland from the Tigris in the West. These were the very canals on which Saddam's regime had built huge pumping stations, which would eventually drain the wetlands and dry the Marsh Arabs out of existence. Now after the invasion and with the pumping stations shut down or destroyed, once again, water, the life blood of the Marshes, flowed through the reed covered channels and the man made canals, Mike had seen by comparing the old satellite imagery against the new photos that gradually the land was returning to its natural state.

Finding the right entrance would not be so easy; the lads all had positions plugged into their GPS that would take them to an area that Mike had estimated as being one of the larger entrances. The maps that the guys were using were taken from American Military maps the information was at least a couple of years old, when the area was still dammed and the regime was still busy pumping the water away, so it had been much dryer, and often hard to marry-up information on the map and that on the Satellite photo's which were not of a great quality.

Mike looked at his GPS the entrance was a little under 5 km, and they were making 10 knots which wasn't too bad considering the weight in the canoe. The GPS gave an estimated time to go as 29 minutes, it was still a long time and anything could happen, Mike lifted his NVG's up and took a sweep of the water ahead, then down his right side, nothing was showing, over the stern, where he could see Jons' Zodiac and the Canoe, the children were all laying down in the bottom, he could make out the tops of a couple of heads protruding above the wooden hull, but couldn't make out any faces, he wondered what they were thinking, had they been rescued or taken hostage, he wondered if they knew the difference, he didn't really know himself.

Mike kept scanning the water around him, the green light through the scope had made his right eye nearly blind in the night. As he took the scope away, all he could see was a black circle, to see clearly without it he had to close his right eye and used his left. He looked back again, Col was still playing with the radio, and Marco was concentrating on what was ahead, checking over his shoulder at the following craft every minute or so. Mike selected the lamp button and the back light glowed on the screen of his GPS, 3km, 16 minutes to go, they were close, but still no aircraft, and as they got closer they would have to slow down, so it was more like 20 maybe 25 minutes.

Mike looked ahead again, and saw a flicker of light; he placed the monocular against his right eye again. He watched as lights flashed in the distance, flaring green through the scope. Mike pulled out the Thermal imager, to get a different view 'I think we've got trouble'

'What, something up there?' Col lifted his head from the radio bag.

Marco didn't hear Mike because of the engine noise 'what's up Col?'

Mike held up a hand to silence the guys, and scanned ahead, he could see 3 white dots moving through the reeds. Mike needed to warn everyone so he used the personal radios, 'Yeah we got company, 3 white hot engines, moving left to right, at 1 O'clock, coming through the reeds'

Jons voice had a tone of worry 'shall I release the tow?'

'No no one do anything yet, they may not be hostile, and we may be able to cut ahead of them, but be ready' Mike crossed his fingers, he knew in his mind that they were going to turn out hostile, and he knew they would be lucky to get away with it again.

He was on the radio again 'OK guys, standby, when they turn we have about 5 minutes, Jon you head straight to the RV, only release the kids if you have to, Gris and I will stay between you and them, use smoke if you can, understood?'

'Roger' Gris

'Roger' Jon

'Roger mate' Marco

'Were fucked' Sven

Mike watched as the 3 white dots got bigger, he then saw the less bright white dots that were heads. There were 2 or 3 people in each boat, almost definitely all armed, Mike switched to the green glow of his rifle sight.

'OK guys they are now heading straight at us definitely armed and hostile, Jon keep going, Gris stay on our right, Marco come round 20 degrees to starboard, and hit the throttle, let's take the fuckers on, good luck guys'

Only Jon replied, 'roger, see you at Babs'

Mike planned to aim slightly left of the 3 craft now heading towards him. He planned to try to hide Jons boat which was going a lot slower from the enemy and at the same time take the fight to them. If they tried to run, or got split up they were outgunned and defiantly dead.

'OK Col, I want smoke in about 2 minutes, spread out all down the Port side'

Smoke was underused at night but as it was as good at night as in the daytime, the main problem was it was the old stuff that didn't float' he had asked for the newer type canister at the stores, and when asked why the Army Quarter Master had laughed thinking he was joking, 'floating smoke!' so guys had kept the non buoyant grenades in their foam packaging with some black tape, and this did the trick.

The 3 craft were now very close, Mike carefully aimed at the lead boat, on the front was a man with a green glow against his face. 'They got a night vision, OK Col, smoke' Mike pulled the trigger and fired, it was hard to acquire a good aim, but Mike pulled the trigger twice each time he had the guy in the centre of his reticule.

On his right he saw tracer wizzing toward the second boat that was fanning out on their side. The third craft was still a little way behind, and still directly behind the lead boat. Col moved up onto Mikes right side, he didn't have a night sight, and was waiting until they were closer. 'Smokes gone, I saved one more in-case we need it later'

'OK mate, you not see yet?'

'no, but I'll let them know when I can'

'OK, if you come to my left then, and concentrate on the driver and engine, I'll get the guy with the scope'

Col moved around and waited for the larger target to come into view. Mike didn't want to waste too much ammunition, so was trying to be careful with his shots.

The small boat was bouncing around so much, 'OK guys, on the count of 3 stop and everyone put down concentrated fire, understood'

'Roger' Gris

'Roger' Marco

'OK 1…2…3, all stop'

The boats stopped within their own length, and now Mike had a steady platform and a good aim, he fired 8 rounds in pairs in rapid succession.

The green light disappeared and so did the man holding it as he splashed into the water. Cols tracer was also finding its target, and the coxswain had turned the boat to face them, hoping to hide under the higher swept bow.

On the other side Gris and Sven were firing so fast it sounded almost like automatic fire. The tracer was making the canoe drive erratically. Marco didn't need to be told to get them on the move again, 'OK, Hold ON' the boat lurched forward as Marco manoeuvred it away from the sharp bows that were speeding towards them.

The third canoe was also closing, and in the distance Mike could see the glow of white water appearing from the reeds as more were coming to join the hunt.

Sven was on the radio, 'we got him, enemy in the water, watch the canoe its outta control'

'OK, well done guys, but we got at least 2 more coming from the river, close on us and lets get out of here' Mike knew that there would certainly be more behind them 'Col let's get this twat' Mike motioned toward the speeding canoe.

Mike and Col both got into firing positions on the right side of the boat, Marco swung the boat so that the canoe would pass down that side. 'watch out for our guys on the other side' they would have to be quick, the coxswain was blind to their manoeuvre at the moment, but it wouldn't be long before they saw each other. Mike had his scope steady on the side of the canoe, and followed the outline down towards the stern. As the profile of the boat changed he saw his target, at that moment the rabbit looked back at the hunter. Mike could see the surprise on his face, as the short man leaned on the tiller of the outboard to conduct a high speed turn and escape, Mike squeezed his trigger, firing 4 deliberate rounds, Col fired almost simultaneously, the rabbit fell backwards, and over the side.

Marco saw the splash of the driver as he hit the water and turned the rubber boat to the North East again. Mike and Col moved towards the back of the boat and took up new positions, on either tube to balance the boat again. Mike could see Gris coming up from behind, 'ease back a little mate, let them catch up' Mike pressed his send button, 'well gone guys, come up on our Port side, I see canoe three has stopped but not for long, and 2, no 3 more coming up from 5 O'clock'

Mike watched as the third canoe, which seemed to be hesitating at a distance, was now picking up speed and renewing it pursuit, obviously spurred on by the other local craft now appearing from behind.

Mike heard a lull in the Outboards revs, making his heart miss a beat, something was wrong. 'Col, quick swap my fuel leads'

Col leaned over and swapped the connection to the next bag, 'that bag doesn't seem very empty mate, you sure its fuel!'

'no I'm not, let's hope the same lowest bidder that made your radios' didn't make the engines eh'

'no they're good engines, we'll be fine' Mike wasn't sure he really felt as positive as he tried to sound.

The engine continued to cough and spluttered; when it did the boat would slow and then suddenly speed up again. Every time it did Mikes heart skipped a beat.

Marco shouted, the anxiety he was now feeling clear in his voice, 'Col, pump the fuel lead, see if it helps'

Gris was now up on their left, but the third canoe was closing, up ahead he could make out Jon and the canoe, it wasn't as far ahead as he had hoped.

The canoe was now on the stern and about 50 meters away, the other 2 canoes were also closing fast.

Mike sat on the collar of the boat and aimed his rifle once again. He followed the lines of the canoe down looking for a target, every now and then he saw the coxswain. Mike waited, waiting for the shot. Then from nowhere tracer was flying across the boat, both green and red, Mike switched left as Col was shouting, 'it's coming from the bow' and returned fire.

Mike leaned out over the boat to get a better shot, when a bright green light flared in his right eye and he felt a dull thud as spasms like electric shocks made his fingers suddenly extend uncontrollably, then he was very cold, cold and wet. He gasped and nearly choked on the strange tasting water, in his mouth and nose. He struggled, kicking his legs arms reaching out and flailing at the water. The noise around him was of high pitched propellers, it sounded like he was going to be run over any second.

The pain in his shoulder was excruciating, he could hardly move his right arm, yet he had too to stay afloat and stay alive. He had to get some air into his life jacket; he was struggling to stay afloat. If he pulled the cord to inflate it then it would be too much, designed to keep a man and all his equipment afloat on his back in the open ocean, it would render him almost unable to move, and he would be a sitting duck.

Mike kicked and struggled to stay afloat; he pulled open the manual inflation valve and tried to blow air into the lifejackets bladder. It was not easy as he needed to use his left hand to open the valve, and every time he exhaled he sunk and had to struggle to the surface again. It took several attempts but was beginning to work.

His arm was starting to work again; it must have been just bruised from the impact. He had been shot, but didn't think he was bleeding, something had saved his life, it wasn't his body armour. The Ministry of Defence wouldn't supply the right kind, only one that was too heavy and didn't float so had been left in the bottom of the boat. It was one thing being shot, but if the bullet went through your life jacket so making it inoperable, even if the body armour saved your life, if you went overboard you weren't coming up. It was one gamble too many for most people.

Marco had watched Mike go over, he shouted 'man over board, and turned the boat around. Col was up and looking forward, and he was now on the radio, 'Gris we lost Mike, he was shot, he's in the water, over'

Col looked over and saw Gris turn his boat back around, 'roger mate, can you see him?'

'No we need the thermal optics' Col searched quickly where Mike had been, 'shit he's taken them in with him'

The first of the three canoes was only about 50 meters away, and someone began to open up on them with a light machine gun. Tracer filled the air around the 2 boats as the gunner adjusted his aim. The other 2 boats were also closing fast, Col returned fire at the canoe, then a voice came over the radio, it was distraught but a voice of command 'OK, we have to get to the RV, the kids are the priority' there was a short break and the radio crackled again 'Marco take one loop and if you don't see him we'll have to go on'

It wasn't a decision anyone would have liked to make, but it was made, Marco finished his sweep, and he and Col stared expectantly into the black water, but saw nothing.

The brief search was complete and Col returned fire over the stern at the first canoe as they drove away.

After only four or five minutes they caught up with Jon towing the canoe with the children.

Gris was on the radio again, 'OK guys, not far now. Marco we have to stand and fight again, and give Jon a chance to get to the shore'

The two craft turned again, they knew they were out gunned and didn't stand much of a chance especially against 3 craft. Col watched as the first canoe circled away for a moment, waiting for his two companions to join him to finish the kill.

Col watched as the three craft now spread out together and ploughed towards them, the wash from the bows spraying in the air as they pitched forward.

Gris's voice was steady and reassuring 'OK guys let them get closer, we don't have much ammo left so make it count'

The hint taken Col changed his magazine, and waited. Marco had turned the boat again, and had his rifle in his hands. 'How many mags you got left?'

'Two full'

'Here take 2 of mine, I haven't used any yet' Marco handed across two full magazines

'Well let's hope we don't need bayonets ah!'

'Let's hope not mine's mounted on a piece of wood above my Dad's bar!'

The radio crackled again, 'OK, standby lads, the left boats yours Marco, and well share the middle one, 10 rounds rapid fire, on my call'

They waited, Col felt the tension building, his finger on the trigger, he watched through his sight as the 3 boats closed, almost enticing him to pull the trigger. It would only be a waste of ammunition, the effect of them all firing concentrated shots would hopefully take a few down, and at the same time make them turn away under the heavy fire.

'Steady guys, a few more seconds, 10 rounds only, rapid....FIRE!'

The tracer filled the space between the enemy boats, the craft skitted from side to side as the coxswains were obviously surprised by the weight of fire, and tried to avoid it. The craft split, and spread out in 3 different directions, just the effect that Gris had hoped for. But within only a few minutes they were re organised and beginning another run, and this time more spread out.

Col looked at Marco who looked as surprised as he felt, 'shit now were in trouble, they must have radios?'

The guys prepared themselves as the radio hissed again, it was Gris 'Jons made it, we can see him ashore, lets go!'

Marco lowered his weapon and grabbed the tiller, 'thank god for that lets get the fuck outta here' Marco revved the engine and the boat heeled over and Col got into a position so he could cover the rear again, and the approaching craft. They were gaining fast now, there was no way they could make it to the shore first. Col tried to take a few shots but with the bouncing of the boat it was just wasting valuable ammunition.

Then the automatic fire began to splash around them again, the tracer streaked from the right hand boat, its size making it a steadier firing platform that the smaller rubber boat, as the machine gun opened up again directly behind them.

The gunner was getting better and some of the bursts were getting too close.

Then a steady stream of red tracer arc its way over their heads and directly into the middle boat, it seemed to be coming from above. Marco looked up, 'Col, its the Chinook!'

The helicopter was hovering in position and the RAF gunner was firing burst after burst at the canoes. He was concentrating on the biggest threat first which was the craft with the machine gun in it. The tracer was finding its mark, and the boat leaned drastically over to starboard to try to escape at high speed, but the movement continued and it rolled over. The engine over revved as the propeller spun in the open air before dying in a puff of smoke, the wooden boat floated upside down just on the surface, then the stern slipped under leaving the very bow pointing out of the water like a tomb stone, above the dead machine gunner and coxswain.

The Chinook now flew in low above their heads, the down draught from the two sets of rotors spraying water all around them as it approached the landing site. With the radio down there was no way of telling the pilot they needed time to look for Mike.

Breakfast at Babs'

The two remain craft beached onto the edge of the reed line at almost the same time. Gris ran forward with Sven to where Jon and Ginge were waiting with the children. Marco and Col stayed by the water's edge watching for enemy.

The children were all huddled together and shaking with fear, Sven had his weapon up, and put his arm on the shoulder of the oldest boy, who pushed it away.

Gris was firmly in charge and formulating a plan for their extraction to the helicopter which was landing somewhere behind them. He needed to ensure that nothing was left behind.

'OK Ginge, remember those grenades we told you not to ever take out of your pouche?'

'Ahh.. yeh'

'Remember how to use one?

'I think so, twist and pull throw and fuckin duck, if I remember your instructions exactly!'

Well yes, except this time don't duck, don't miss and run away sharpish, OK?

Col had been collecting his satellite radio from the boat, 'OK Gris ready to go, are you sure about this, a Matloe with a gun is bad enough but a red phos grenade, must be the first one in history!'

'Oh fuck off' Ginges reply had a nervous edge to it, Gris could see he wasn't comfortable, but knew when he went back to the Navy it would be a story he would tell his ship mates for the rest of his career.

'he'll have to do, I need everyone that can shoot straight to cover us'

'OK guys, as soon as the grenades go off Sven you take the kids, everyone else in pairs back to the chopper, OK Ginge go do it'

It seemed that the machine gun fire from the Chinook had given them some breathing space, but with the chopper now obviously landing Gris could make out green shadows emerging through his NVG's. 'Ginge get a fuckin move on, OK Guys 2 enemy craft dead ahead, closing fast, Sven get those kids moving'

'OK, Im gone' Sven was up and pulling the boy with him, hoping the rest would follow, but non moved 'come on come on, yella, yella, let's go' the children were like sheep and once one or two began to move they all ran with Sven toward the noise of the helicopter.

Gris was watching the craft approaching, once the grenades went off they would be shielded from the enemy, this could be their last chance to take some down, and give them the time they needed. OK anyone with a clear shot get some rounds down, just watch out for...'

It was not really a text book fire control order and he never got to complete it before both automatic and single shots rang out from the team, he was sure that they knew he was going to say watch out for Ginge.

The sudden sound of rounds, muzzle flashes and tracer whizzing past his head had caused Ginge to dive for cover, but he soon recovered and hastened in his task. He pulled out 3 grenades and laid them on the ground in front of himself, he wasn't going to fuck this up. Methodically he pulled the pins, threw the grenades into each boat and ran.

The burst of phosphorus lit the whole area silhouetting Ginge as he ran back and producing a cloud of instant thick smoke. The smell was sweet but nauseating at the same time and each flare of light and smoke was followed by more conventional explosions as plumes of flames signalled the petrol in the fuel bags combusting.

Gris had an eye closed to try to preserve his night vision, but due to the brightness of the explosions had only been marginally successful.

He took charge again, shouting his command over the noise of the burning craft and weapons firing, 'CEASE FIRE...... in pairs, back to the helo, MOVE'.

The guys moved back in two's towards the helicopter, one always covering the other moving. After the blinding light of teh grenades it was difficult to see what was ahead or underfoot. As Gris made it to the chopper and before getting on board he finally looked around to make sure no one was left, in the distance he saw the 3 men appear in the light of the burning boats. They were blinded by the light and were firing in the general direction of the noise of the helicopter, luckily with little hope for success.

Gris ensured he was last on over the ramp, down the right hand side in the dim light he could see the children, the guys were strapping them in. He sat on the left, at the rear, and grabbed the headphones from the Aircrewman.

'We have a man down, back over towards the North east entrance'

One of the Pilots answered Marco's plea, 'OK but we only have 40 mins fuel and we need 20 to get back'

'What about the Lynx?'

'What Lynx, were it, we'll do our best, but 20 minutes is all we have, where did you last see him'

The helo was lifting off Marco was desperate, Mike was still out there somewhere, 'OK put us back down'

'Sorry fellas, weve got to get you back, but well come back as soon as we can'

'OK, he went overboard between where you shot the canoe and the Northern ERV' Gris knew the pilot had the Northern emergency rendezvous point marked on his map, and it was in the general direction.

Gris leaned over to Col and shouted into his ear, 'we've only got 20 minutes fuel, were going to do a search, move down to the ramp, or a window use your NVG's, pass it on'

Col nodded, and Gris swung around to look over the tail gate, his weapon ready so that he could use his sight to search. In the distance he could see the glow of the burning boats and wondered if Mike was still alive and if he could see them too.

The Chinook made several sweeps of the area, but they had seen nothing, the lake looked eerily black and still, as if the events of the past few hours had never happened.

The end of the 20 minutes was signalled by a conversation between the pilot and co pilot 'OK, that's it I'm afraid, come round to 265, clear right…sorry Corporal but that's it' Gris's heart sunk, 'are there no more assets?'

'Not my call I'm sorry, we have informed Zero, its up to them'

It was no use pleading, and Gris knew they could not go straight back in as they had nothing left, they had to get back now, re equip themselves, get more ammunition and get back out here, the sooner the better. He looked around at the looks on the guys faces, now more than ever they needed a leader. Mike was not here and he would have to do it, take charge, re-organise and lead them back out to find Mike.

He shouted again into Cols ear, 'were coming straight back, tell the lads' Col held his thumb up and nodded, the word went around, and one by one the guys looked at him and nodded or gave a thumbs up, before sinking back into their own thoughts.

Chapter 8
Alone

It had already been a long night, luckily and to Mike's relief and surprise the round that had throw him from the boat had ricochet off his own gun and the force had been enough to dive the butt of his gun into his shoulder, unbalance him on the wildly manoeuvring Zodiac and throw him over board. When he had come back to the surface the enemy boats were almost on top of him, but they passed him chasing the Zodiacs and Canoe, harassing them as they made for the rendezvous. Mike knew as he watched the chase move away from him, that he had to be left behind.

The last hour or so he had been mad at himself for losing his balance, for leaning too far out, or standing too high to try to get a clear shot. The worst bit had been hearing the Chinook fly directly over him, then seeing it come down and engage the enemy boats, rounds were flying everywhere, the tracer lighting up the night had been too much for the 2 remaining skiffs and they had at first retreated to the reeds. He then heard the two engines roar as the helicopter landed to collect the others, and watched the exchange of gunfire. His heart sunk with a feeling of dread as the grenades exploded and watched in anguish as the boats burned, knowing now his only chance was the Chinook. When it took off again they had searched the area for about 10 minutes but then it had disappeared into the night. He listened as the thud of the rotors had faded and they had left him for dead, after all he had done for them, they hadn't even tried that hard to look for him, fuckers. Mike was angry with himself, and the guys, but he knew he needed to sort himself out, there was no one to blame, he had to survive, the rescue would come and come soon. Once the helicopter had gone the water became alive with boats they knew he was out here, he was sure they had seen him fall out, he now had to get as far from the area as he could, he had swam towards the bank and the cover of the reeds and intended to follow the edge for as far as possible

The Chinook had only made a brief search, but it was looking in the area that he had first fallen over board, no one would see him in this dark water. In his kit he had a strobe that flashed an Infa Red light invisible to the naked eye, which the searching pilots and anyone else with night vision goggles would see for miles. Unfortunately the top had been smashed by the force of the bullet or maybe his own weapon smashing against it, it had become waterlogged and useless. He also had a small torch in his kit but the chopper was too far away, and there were boats everywhere, as the Chinook began its search they were all pretending to fish or were hiding in the reeds, but they were between him and the helicopter, he couldn't risk it, there would be another chance he was sure.

Mike had swum for about an hour now, and he had blown a little more air into his lifejacket to help him cope with the weight of his water logged equipment, he was now in a small channel, on both sides reeds towered high above him. It was time to find some cover to wait out the rest of the night and try to prepare for the rescue attempt, that would surly come, the thing to do was lay low and stay positive, any thoughts of being forgotten were to be immediately dismissed, the lads would be here as soon as they could. It was a huge area but it was only a matter of time. Mike could see that just ahead the river split into 2, a junction or maybe a small island, even with the moonlight it was hard to make out, that should be a safe place for now, get some cover and lay low.

Mike saw movement on the water, about 10 meters from him a small head could be seen just above the water, a small reptile, it was swimming towards him, maybe a terrapin, then he saw the long tail, shit a snake, heading directly for him at eye level. Mike made a splash in the water with an outstretched hand to try to scare it away, it did the opposite and woke the snake up to a possible threat, now the snake was only a few meters away, its tail making wider motions on the water. About half a meter long, dark, and with a wide head, Mike had seen only pictures before, a water cobra, aggressive and very venomous. Instead of swimming away it adopted an aggressive stance, pulling its pointed head back and into a striking position, Mike froze. His Dad had always told him that a snake is more scared of you, well Mike could see its small sharp black eyes, this bastard wasn't half as scared as he was.

Any movement now and it would be all over, he would rather have come face to face with an armed militia. The snake was not going to back down and any movement in the water with all his heavy waterlogged kit on would be too slow to escape the strike, and mean a slow death from the deadly venom. Well Mike had already decided he wasn't going to die in the corner of some fucked up foreign field. He took a short sharp but quiet breath and sank onto his knees, using his arms to force himself down, as his head plunged under the water dragged down by the weight of his kit he saw the sharp, swift movement as the cobra expanded and lunged forward to kill, he felt the jaw brush the top of his head, and ducked as deep as he could. With a push forward he half swam and half stumbled under the water for what seemed like an age but was in reality about half a minute, slowly he came to the surface, grabbing the underwater section of a reed to help him to the surface, the Cobra had made its escape.

He didn't want to experience that again, it was time to find some good old safe dry land.

Mike could see the edges of a levee, the top edge of which was silhouetted by the moonlight, and was becoming discernable through the reeds. Up ahead the pale light was glinting off of the spans of a bridge. Mike swam on, only making slow progress, the current was getting stronger where the river was being channelled between the bridge supports, every movement was now becoming more and more of a struggle. Mike was feeling tired, it was time to get on dry land

Coming into focus in the dark and just short of the bridge was a small hut, it appeared to be only half built, or maybe half demolished, but may provide somewhere safe and dry to rest for a while, and recover some energy. Mike also needed to think carefully and plan his next move.

The hut had a door facing the river and looked very inviting, Mike made it to the river bank only 20 meters from the bridge. Mike looked up in the dark at the Bridge from a distance it had looked unpretentious, from almost below it looked intimidating, girders of steel and concrete slabs towering above him.

The banks were steep and slippery, he was finding it impossible to get a grip and drag himself out. Ten metres or so downstream Mike saw a small clump of short reeds and grass. He swam down and used most of his remaining reserves of energy to drag himself from the water and onto the slippery bank. Grabbing at reed, grass, and clumps of dirt, anything to help drag himself and his heavy, water laden kit from the water. With a final show of effort he crawled slowly into the hut, his wet kit now caked in sand and mud. In the small building the floors were covered in old urine soaked straw, and almost completely carpeted in goat facieses, the smell was acrid and burnt his nose with every breath, exhausted Mike leaned against the wall. Unable to find the strength to move he decided he would close his eyes for a few minutes rest, and then re-plan his escape.

It was the sounds of an engine that woke Mike up, the sun was up, light was probing through what was left of the thatched roof, and the wide gap where the door should have been.

Mike could hear Arab voices very close by, the sound of a man talking excitedly, then the more subtle reply of a women. Not wanting to compromise his position Mike stayed still, just listening, he looked at his watch it was just gone 6:30am he couldn't believe he had slept for the last 2 hours or so and not woken up, but he felt better for it.

There was no way he could move in day light, he could hear a helicopter buzzing around but it was very faint and sounded like it was coming from the South, the stream must have brought him further North than he had intended. It wouldn't help the searchers; he'd opened the gap between where he was expected to be and where he actually was.

Surly the area would be swarming with troops soon, but Mike knew the risks with the job when he has said he could do it. With the elections and all the recent problems with insurgents the resources were limited, and only one troop in support, it was a huge area to cover with less than 30 men and 5 or 6 vehicles. They would be hard pushed to even cover the 4 Emergency Rendezvous which is where the search would start, followed by every possible hiding place that Mike could be, and of course no one could be sure that he was still alive. They probably thought they were looking for a body; he had to do this alone.

Mike knew he would have to move as soon as darkness fell, but now rested, he felt hungry and a little weak. He was becoming dangerously curious about what was around him, what was outside the hut. Slowly and cautiously he eased himself out through the door, the first danger was the bridge that over looked him; although the angle was probably too acute for someone crossing it to look down, especially if he went out of the door to the left, and around the back of the hut.

Mike lay on the ground, and carefully looked around the corner of the hut, there was a little girl sat on her own with her back to Mike, about 20 meters away, she was sat on a low wall that led down to another small hut. Meandering around her were several goats, a mix of white and brown in colour and all very scraggy. Mike thought they looked how he felt. Suddenly out of the hut appeared a women, Mike ducked back and heard the women called to the little girl, who answered, then the women called again, but the difference in pitch told Mike that she had turned away and way probably heading back inside. So he carefully sneaked around again, this time the girl was looking straight at him, he froze, shit. She was about 8 maybe 9, and wearing a very simple light blue dress and scarf, Mike froze, just watching, the girl smiled gently and walked away.

Mike heard the noise of a car on the bridge as it rattled over the timber boards, he pulled back, not quite sure whether to stay or run, the car turned down off the bridge and Mike saw the dust as it pulled up outside the hut.

Mike waited, he stayed close to the corner by the door, he had found a piece of timber just outside and was ready in-case of compromise, if anyone walked through the door they would get it square in the face, he also had his pistol, but the sound of a shot would bring armed men from every village in the area, and that would not help his survival chances.

The midday sun was now at its zenith, and the air was hot to breath, burning Mike's throat as he carefully and quietly drew it in.

Mike heard the vehicle turn down towards his hiding place, and pull up sharply not far from the Hut, it was obviously in a hurry, he had found a small loophole in the wall that looked over toward the small home, the white pickup was full of men all armed, young and old, there was a lot of shouting, everyone was excited, one old man was pointing first down the river that Mike had swum last night, then to his relief to the west, away from his current location but towards the emergency rendezvous he was hoping to get too, the other man from the hut stepped out, wearing a blue chequered shirt with a dark red stain on the upper arm, Mike looked again he recognised those eyes immediately, it was the same guy from the canoe last night.

Somehow unlike his friends, the enemy knew he was alive, and now they were searching for him. It would only be a matter of time, they probably controlled the villages, they knew the land and they knew where he had gone over, the odds were now definitely against him making it out.

From the entrance to the hut the little girl appeared, the man with the shirt knelt and spoke to her, she replied in her soft Arabic, he placed a hand on her head nodded and smiled.

He turned towards Mikes peep hole, Mikes heart stopped as he seemed to look straight into the small hole that Mike was watching through. Mike dared not breath and waited for the shouting. It never came.

Instead the man looked away, and shouted at the driver of the pickup pointing out over the bridge, he climbed in through the passenger side, and pushed the other passenger into the middle. The door slammed shut, and the pickup reversed out, turning back up toward the bridge and in a cloud of sand sped off. Mike felt the relief overwhelm him, for the moment at least he was safe.

Mike crawled back into the hut, he noted with despair that the pickup was going in the same direction he needed to go, the only advantage at the moment was they were busy running around looking for him, and he was resting in the last place they would look, he needed to save all of his energy for tonight. Unfortunately Mike knew that it would only be a matter of time before someone stumbled across him then he was in a whole world of shit. He had to move, and the sooner the better.

Mike eased himself around the corner again to take a look, he scanned the hut first. There was a small square opening for a window. A light silk cloth of white and blue was hanging over it, the breeze causing it to gently flutter. Behind the silk was a shadow, moving gently, probably the mother working in her kitchen.

Mike looked passed the hut, there, only about 20 metres away was a small drainage ditch that led back into the reeds. This was Mikes escape route, it would get him clear of the village, and although not in the right direction for the rendezvous at least away from the enemy search party for now.

He began to crawl very slowly toward the ditch, crawling on the hard packed sand was hurting his knees and elbows, feeling the sharp pain with every movement. He was so close to the hut now, any noise could give him away; he began to wish he hadn't started. Mikes heart was racing as he crawled on, the corner of the hut approaching. Suddenly something moved he glanced over, then a loud squawking noise, Jesus though Mike, four geese were coming towards him, his only chance was back. As he backed away, the noise from the Geese, although not yet directed at him, reminded Mike of ringing Church bells in a small English church warning the whole village of an invasion of German Paratroopers. Out of the corner of his eye the silk lifted in the breeze, and he slipped carefully back into the out building.

He leaned back against the wall, and could see the Geese loiter just outside the door. Shit, guarded by 4 Geese and not a thing he could do. Mike decided to sit tight for a while, no point making any rash decisions, he knew if he panicked he was dead.

Mike looked at his watch it was nearly 2 he had not seen or heard any more movement. In the past hour a few cars had driven across the bridge he had heard the thump thump thump as the vehicles wheels had rattled over the wooden slats, but thankfully non had stopped.

Breakfast at Babs'

Mike began to think of home, his family, in particular his mother who would be idly working in the garden or feeding one of her menagerie of Horses, rabbits goats or chickens, he had often used her image to calm himself it gave him a link with the real world, the place where he intended to be one day, he drifted to sleep.

He awoke with a jump, a hand was on him, he pushed back against the wall and hit his head against the dried wattle. She jumped too, the little girl fell back in the mud and ended up in a sitting position just in front of him. She looked scared, and was holding the tail of her light blue silk scarf over her face. Mike was sorry he had reacted so violently, and tried his best smile. It worked and the little girl let the scarf go and smiled back.

In front of him was a red scarf tied in a bundle. The little girl pointed at it, and then at her mouth. Mike leaned forward and opened the bundle, inside was a browning green apple, some dates, a small bottle of water that although marked as still water had long since been drunk and was filled with local water, but Mike could purify it in a 20 minutes, lastly and to Mikes surprise a foil packet that he recognised, the English print was only just visible, Fruit Dumplings in Butter Scotch Sauce. Of all the puddings that came with the British rations this was the worse, Mike had only ever met one marine who even ate them and that was Sven, but he would eat anything. The Army had obviously been through here and given away all their unwanted rations to the kids, and even they didn't want it. Still it was high calorie food, and it was just the sugar rush that Mike needed. He looked up to smile again at the little girl who had showed so much humanity, but she was already disappearing through the door.

The food made Mike feel a lot better; he was no longer tired and meant that he could save his few emergency rations that he had left in his kit for later. The bar of chocolate, which would by now be misshaped by the heat, and the boiled sweets he would need for tonight.

Chapter 9
On the Run

Mike looked at his watch, it was a little after 5, and the comfort of darkness would soon come. He began to imagine his funeral, who would come, and how long people would remember him. He had lost mates, and sometimes he had to force himself to think of them, to remember them, give them a little of his time. He always felt guilty during the annual remembrance service, during the two minutes silence he would go through the guys he had know and had died, some in conflict, but more often than not on a Motorbike, or from a stupid accident, he would feel terrible when he realised it had been a year since he had thought of them last.

He had hoped to become renowned enough one day to have a space in the Times obituaries. However these days your past successes in life were determined by how quickly you were immortalised by a mobile phone joke, Mike smiled at the thought.

Well he was not going to get in the Times yet, so he would have to get out of this mess. Through the door he watched as the huge orange ball rested momentarily on the horizon, before finally disappearing in one swift movement. It darkened almost immediately, and at last night fell, it was time for Mike to make his move. Mike took the last sip from the sterilised water in the plastic bottle, he must be thirsty as he could not taste the usual iodine aftertaste. Mike checked his equipment and re-secured the chest clips that he had undone earlier to aid venting, trying to keep himself cool. He had one last bottle of water in his kit, 1½ litres, he had to try to get through the cool night without needing too much of it.

Mike had decided that as the Southern landing site had been used last night, the enemy may not consider that any alternatives were very far, and would concentrate on the area between the river and this and any other possible landing site to the South. He would head North to the third and most Northerly ERV. The only problem was that according to the Satellite imagery it was the only possible extraction point in the Northern area and so may be guarded easily by a small group. It was also planned so that it would have easy access from the lake, and not easily reinforced from land. If Mike was to go all the way down to it, and found it guarded, or the terrain impassable he may be caught out and run out of time.

Mike eased himself from his hiding place, and decided the best way to move initially away from the dwellings was by the river. He slipped into the cool water once again, this time he wasn't wearing his life jacket, but was using it as a floatation device held out in-front of him. It was no good going up stream under the bridge, there was bound to be more houses along the banks, and also the stream was being channelled as the river passed under the bridge this would mean Mike would use up vital strength fighting against the current.

The stream was moving gently down this side of the bank and Mike didn't have to work very hard as he allowed himself to drift for a few hundred metres. Then on his left the reeds parted, and Mike found himself crawling up on to a cleared area where a track came down to the river. The vegetation had been cut back in a large square, in the middle of which were large square piles of bundled reeds, these were obviously the cultivated during the day waiting for trucks to transport them to market. Leaning against these piles were several flat bottomed boats, Mike moved carefully forward investigating the boats and wondering about taking one down river, they didn't have engines but it may be worth a try. He was still weighing up the odds, and walking around the small boats when he saw a vehicle. A small white Toyota pickup was parked next to the bundles. Mike tried the door and it opened, he looked inside and couldn't believe his luck, the keys were in the ignition. The owner must still be on the water; Mike stepped in and held his breath as he turned the key. The car started straight away, looking at the fuel gauge it was hall full. Mike put it in into drive and drove off down the track.

The road was taking him North West, Mike started to imagine driving straight out of the marshes and up to the front gates of the camp. He began to smile to himself, as he saw the faces of Marco, Sven and the lads as they laughed and took the piss. The track was empty and rose up above the reeds onto a levee, in the far distance he could see twinkling lights. Then two lights appeared directly ahead, coming straights at him, there was nowhere to hide, he couldn't get off the levee, and the track was only just wide enough for 2 cars. Mike had been driving carefully with his lights off; he now turned them on, and looked around inside the car. The dash and facia were covered in a grey velvet type fur, he pulled and ripped at it, only lightly glued to the plastic it came off almost in one whole strip, Mike now wrapped the material inside out around his head and over his mouth. Steering with his left hand, Mike felt for the handle of his pistol and hoped.

The lights from the approaching car were getting brighter, he could almost make out the occupants, as they were about to pass Mike flicked his beam on a couple of times hoping to blind them a little, and held up his hand, hoping the camouflage cream would make him look dark skinned.

Breakfast at Babs'

Mike cringed as the passenger stared at him, Mike looked away and drove on his heart truly in his mouth, watching his mirrors waiting for the brake lights to come on, to Mike's relief they didn't, and the car disappeared down the track. Mike then had another worry, what about when they get down the end of the track and meet up with the real owner of the car. Mike sped up as much as he dared, but although the track was dead straight it was very loose, and every now and then a large sections had slipped away.

He guessed he had driven about 5 or 6 km now, he wished he had noted the odometer, or reset the trip in case he needed to know late. His lights caught something ahead on the levee, it was a pickup, his lights had caught the driver's side window. It was parked across the road with its side lights on, it was deliberate, and was clearly a check point and road block. He saw the cab light come on as someone stepped out. Mike knew he wouldn't be able to talk his way out with 5 words of Arabic one of which meant bread; he had no option but to drive through. Lifting his foot off of the accelerator he began to slow up a little as he approached, there were 3 men, 2 were carrying Kalashnikovs, the third was sat in the back of the pickup, and he had an RPG, which was now trained in Mike's direction. He had to get as close as he could before he made his move, his main problem was the RPG, but it needed about 20 metres to arm and if the operator was not trained another 30 seconds or so to re load and have another pop. Mike needed him to waste his first shot.

As Mike approached he dropped the shift on the automatic to D2 it should give him the power and torque he needed to pull this off. The Iraqi by the cab was now holding his hand up, and had his AK47 levelled in his right hand, he still had the element of surprise, he was about 30 metres from the truck as the character holding up his hand took an almost theatrical double take, obviously he recognised the car, and that the driver was not the old bearded man he expected to see. Shit, it was too soon,

Mike pulled on the full beam to give him light and hopefully blind his enemy, and pushed his foot to the floor. The engine laboured as he pushed the peddle down hard, Mike held his breath as the car slowly built up power. The Iraqi now has his AK 47 in the shoulder, and began shouting, on the back the man with the RPG had shouldered it and was now pointing it at Mike's car. Mikes heart missed a beat as he saw the flash of the RPG fire; he swerved to the right and aimed to collide with the lighter rear end of the pickup. The projectile smashed through the rear passenger window and Mike flinched as a rush of air hit the back of his head as it continued out through the window out the other side.

The left side of his bonnet smashed into the pickup, and the momentum was just enough to carry him through, as Mike revved away he looked in his mirror, the brakes on the pickup were obviously not serviced as it rolled forwards and over the levee into the marsh. On the back a flash made Mike's heart stop as the RPG was fired again, the operator was not so green, and if he hadn't been in the lunging pickup, would probably have hit Mike's car. Mike ducked as the projectile hit the pickups roof, glancing off and detonating several seconds later on the road 15 Metres in front of him, splinters hit the car and the windscreen frosted in front of him. Mike breathed a sigh of relief and punched through the glass making a hole large enough for him to see. He drove on through the flames left by the TNT, but his engine was making dreadful clunking noises, the collision with the truck, and the shrapnel from the RPG had taken their toll. Without warning the motor over revved, but the car didn't go any faster. In fact to Mike's horror he was slowing down. So much for driving all the way back and in through the camp gates.

The car came to a halt, and Mike clambered out looking back up the road he saw the RPG man had chased him on foot and was taking aim again. He scrambled down the levee, as he did he heard the whoosh of the rocket and impact as the pickup erupted and was torn apart behind him, the force hit his back and threw him down the slope. At the bottom Mike stood up and ran out into the dark.

After a couple of hundred meters Mike stopped, he was exhausted, he leant over, his hands on his knees as he tried to catch his breath, this was the wrong thing to do he knew he should stay upright to help open his chest and let the oxygen that his body was demanding in to his lungs. He forced himself upright and looked back across the field, in the distance the vehicle was burning bright and the orange light lit up the track he had taken across the field, they were as obvious as moose tracks across fresh snow. He could hear the shouting around the burning car, then a few rounds of automatic fire, Mike thought they probably firing at the car in anger, he also thought for a moment that at least that meant a few less rounds to shoot at him later, Mikes mind was playing games with him, it was stupid really they'd have plenty of rounds if he let them get close enough. Somehow, maybe it was the bright flames, but the group had missed his tracks, but they were now actively looking around for signs of his escape. Mike was exposed and in the open, the only thing darker than him was a 50 cm wide track in the light sand. Probably where a tractor tyre had turned the darker sand over, he lay in it, hopefully his pursuers had looked too long at the blazing pickup and had ruined their night vision. He listened intently, they were still being very noisy but it seemed to be getting quieter. Mike looked up and to his relief they were heading up the road. They were still shouting at each other, but walking in the opposite direction from where Mike was laying. It was time to move again, he hoped he could make some real ground before they caught onto his scent again.

The big decision he now had to make was which direction to go, he could double back, but the risks were great, not much room to manoeuvre between the villages, and too many dogs and geese. To head further West and out into the flat open farm land was also dangerous, the silk map he had made was based on an out of date original, and it obviously wasn't as detailed as he needed, and got vaguer the further from the lake he got, on top of that Mike had a D in Art. He also didn't know how populated that area was or the lay of the land, the only real option was to carry on heading North then East around the lake, and hope to find a search party either on one of the few roads, or to make it eventually to the Helicopter rendezvous.

Mike knew his people would be out looking for him soon, but with the Elections only 2 days away the whole country was probably in turmoil, the military would have its hands full. They probably thought he was already dead, and even if they didn't they probably didn't appreciate the full danger Mike was now in. Mike mentally kicked himself, negative thinking is sure to get you killed, he would make it out, people did care, Gris, Marco, Col, Sven or any of the others wouldn't leave him unless they knew he was definitely dead. Did they think he was already dead, is that why they were so quick to leave him, maybe they thought he had been killed in the fire fight, maybe no one was coming.

No way, they knew he was OK and would return, it was only a matter now of evading his pursuers and finding some where safe to hide and await the Cavalry.

The night was getting colder, the wind was blowing only slightly, but enough to blow through Mikes sweat soaked shirt, a combination of the wind, and his bodies lack of energy meant that Mike was shivering with the cold now. He did not want to stop, his limbs were tired, his head was tired and his mouth was dry. Every now and then Mike would shut his eyes and doze for a few seconds at a time as he walked, it was a bad habit to get into but the exhaustion was taking over. He looked down at his watch, covering the face with his hand he pressed the light button, the face illuminated as Mike tried to focus on the hands, it took several attempts to make sense of the display, he had to stare and force his mind and eyes to work together, it was nearly 4:30, the LCD clock in the car had read 8 just before he had crashed. In 8 and a half hours in full kit at night, even over some unforgiving landscape like Dartmoor he could have easily covered 20 maybe 30 Kilometres, but tonight in his weakened condition, and over this terrain it was probably no more than 6 or 7. He must be within 1 or 2 km of the rendezvous by now, and he was close enough to see if any helicopters came in to the area, he had also crossed at least one of the roads that any ground troops would use to approach the area.

It was time to lay up or die, the problem was where, the best option would be to find some area of reeds near the road, with water around, but shallow enough to run over.
Mike decided to give himself 30 minutes to find somewhere, and if not to stop anywhere remotely suitable.

He could see a levee a few hundred metres to the North East, if he was lucky it was one that bordered the lake, if his calculations were wrong it could mean another night of walking. He could see water glinting in the moonlight, and dark areas that would probably be reeds. As he got nearer the ground sloped away and he was walking through water logged marsh, his feet were sinking with every step. Mike could make out the dark area ahead that he hoped were the reeds, he slogged on step over step, dragging each boot out of the sodden ground, the effort of moving was making every muscle in his body cry out even his jaw was beginning to ach from the effort.

He was now very close and could make out the shape of the reeds, only 20 metres or so and he could take a rest. As he stared towards the reeds something caught his eye, a movement, Mike froze, all the senses that had deserted him for the last few hours returned in a rush of blood to the head and an adrenalin rush that made his head feel light. Not daring to move Mike tried to concentrate on the dark shape that was standing between him and his haven.

Mike reached down to his pistol, he hadn't had it drawn as he had needed his hands and had feared dropping it in the water.

It was in a holster that was stitched on to the left side of his combat vest. The Browning 9mm pistol was secured with a holding strap with Velcro ends, the Velcro, would open with a loud tearing noise. Bastard Velcro, he knew he should have replaced it, but always thought if he needed his pistol it would already be in his hand or drawn from the holster in a hurry, and the tearing noise of the strap would be the least of his worries.

Mike decided to lay still and evaluate his possible enemy first, before making any more moves. Cocking his head towards the shadow he held his breath and listened, making good use of his better right ear, he opened his mouth a little. He could now clearly hear breathing, so he hadn't imagined the movement. He turned his head again, scanning across the area, and not directly at the target.

Mike look slightly off centre, using the rods in his eyes this improved his ability to make out objects, and helped to limit the effects of seeing things move that are not really there, or are not really moving.

He could definitely make out a round shape, a body, but it didn't seem to be moving, he had to be sure what he was facing, and whether he could back out without being heard.

Mike slowly knelt hoping to silhouette the shape against the lightening night sky. Mikes right knee sunk into the marsh, ahead the shadow took on a whole new shape and began to move towards him. Mike struggled to pull himself back up, the mud enveloping his knee. Mike reached out with his left hand grabbing at the base of the reeds to help.

The breathing got louder as the enormous head, body and tusks of a water buffalo, appeared. It began to move toward him, obviously as curious about Mike as he had been about it. Mike had to get around the beast and into the reeds, the adrenaline helped and he moved around the buffalo almost stumbling in the swamp, the Buffalo had now stopped again and watched equally unsure of the strange man hunting in the night.

Mike approached the reeds, trying to do it with caution but the lure of reaching cover and moderate safety making his heart pump so hard and fast he could feel it throbbing against the inside of his combat vest, he splashed through the wet land making more noise than he should, but one side of his brain had chosen to ignore the more sensible side, that told him to tread carefully, the promise of a place to hide and rest was too strong and he trudged as quickly as he could for the last few metres, almost falling across the first line of reeds, he forced himself to push onward through the tall grass for a few more minutes before dropping down on to his back in exhaustion.

The warmth of the sun on his face woke him up, Mike was so tired he had to fight to keep his eyes open, and at first couldn't work out why he was surrounded in thick straw. It took a few seconds before the memories of the previous night came flooding back in to his fatigued mind, after a few more minutes he began to think straight once again. He knew he had to get up and take a look at where he was, and decide how safe he really was. Things always looked different at night and what had seemed like a secure hiding place last night may prove to be quite the opposite in the clear light of day.

Mike knew however the dangers he faced if he was seen and so very carefully raised himself from the ground, and slowly followed the track back through the reeds that he had made last night. The reeds thinned as he neared the edge that he had nearly fallen across last night, Mike lowered himself onto his belly and crawled the last few metres, until he could see out across the Marsh land that he had negotiated that night. Over to his left was a large levee, and on top what was probably a dirt road linking the small villages and damming out the Marsh Lakes. Down the levee Mike saw a glint of light, sun reflected on glass, a vehicle was coming down the road. He guessed still a Kilometre or so away. Mike lowered himself down as far as he could get, at its closes point the road passed about 200 metres from where he was laying, it would be stupid to get seen now. As the vehicle got closer he saw it was a bus, white and red cloths were flying from the vents above the windows, inside it was full of women. They were all singing and oblivious to the curious ragged figure peering from the reeds. One hundred metres or so behind were two battered white pickups, these were over full with men, young and old all shouting and singing, it was a wedding party on its way to the ceremony. Mike watched in seclusion and felt the irony, these people were enjoying a family occasion, the start of a new life, maybe one that wouldn't be so full of hope if guys like Mike hadn't risked their lives and own family happiness; and here he was laying up to his neck in cold, dirty water, running, hiding and fighting for his life…sometimes life was shit.

The vehicles passed without noticing the solitary figure, and Mike was happy as his hiding place now seemed safe enough. He was probably safest near the edge after all, and he would be able to see people coming and still have a little time to react, or hide. Also it would be a good place to try to attract the attention of a friendly helicopter or patrol, something he had to be ready for, and could afford to miss. They must be out there somewhere, why wasn't the place crawling with friendlies by now; he knew why of course, the elections were swamping all the assets. He was now also quite a long way from where he had lost contact from the others. The nearest emergency RV was at least 1 kilometre away maybe a little more, and it was near the waters edge impossible to try to get to in daylight. He just had to sit tight and wait, it would come, and he was sure that the boys were out there somewhere.

Chapter 10
Closing In

Gris was first off of the Chinooks rear ramp as it touched down at the
RV that was closest to where the ambush had taken place 2 nights ago, the
Chinook was going to make a sweep of all the villages and roads, and
check out all the Land RV's. Help was coming, Gris just hoped it wasn't
too late, he had banged on every door all the way up to the Area
Commander. Unfortunately with the fact that the whole area had erupted
in riots and chaos because of the elections, and no one really believing
Mike could really still be alive it had taken 36 hours to redeploy on a search
and rescue mission. Now though a company from the Black Watch was on
its way in Land Rovers after being relieved in place by the Scots Guards
around Al-Amara, they had had a bad night of it, now they were extremely
pissed off that there had been a friendly out on the ground and they had
been too tied up to help.

There were also 2 Scimitars on the way, the Scimitar was a small agile 8
tonne reconnaissance tank equipped with a 30mm Rarden cannon and a

7.62 mm machine gun. The Black Watch were going to provide some extra
fire power if it was needed, and that would be on the scene in 30 minutes
or so, the Vehicles would cover the levee that bounded the lake, centred
on the bridge and overlooking the main village where unknown to anyone
Mike had escaped from earlier that night.

The main problem was that movement by road in an area predominantly
Marshland was that there were very few tracks that were negotiable at any
kind of speed, so progress was very slow. Another major problem was that
since the end of the war all the interlinking bridges, built over the
numerous canals and irrigation ditches by Saddam to carry his Tanks along
this boundary with Iran had been dismantled, over night by gangs of men
armed with cranes, trucks and AK47's and sold for scrap in the markets of
Al-Almara and Baghdad.

The village was quite as the Scimitars took up position, a platoon from
the Black Watch had gone ahead in 4 stripped down Land Rovers and
carrying 4 soldiers each. They were all determined to find the missing
Marine.

Sgt Dean Thomas had been flying his Lynx over every village and every
waterway in the area, all he had achieved so far was to piss off the villagers,
frighten their half starved goats and nearly get him and his crew killed
when a flock of birds suddenly flew out from between the reeds, all he
knew was the Marines had lost a man, and everyone was doing their best to
get him back.

In the distance out to the East he could see the dust clouds as the troops
made their way into the area, Dean looked down at his fuel gauge, and
spoke into his helmet mike 'OK Steve one last run up the Levee then we'll
pick up the Canal and head back, the infantry will be here soon anyway'

'Roger that, this is pointless now anyway, he's long gone, probably never
made it out the water' the Lynx banked over toward the Levee and then
swung North following the road up, in the distance a bus was making its

way towards them followed by some Pickup's, 'there you are Dean a Wedding, that'll be you next summer, except they got more friends than you'

Mike had heard the Lynx in the distance, and held his breath, it was not near enough for him to take the chance and try to attract its attention, now it seemed to turn. He watched with bated breath, he prayed it was turning towards him, this was his only chance, and if it followed the road he would be seen for sure, suddenly the adrenalin began to flow, he could feel the energy he so desperately needed surging through his body. The Lynx was turning down the road, it was low, and if it passed it couldn't fail to miss him, he ran out from the reeds and began to shout and wave, the Lynx continued to fly the same course. It would surly see him any minute, then to his left up on the Levee he saw the bus appear again, he could see the Women again still singing their wedding songs, and flying home made flags out of the windows, the noise of their singing was drowned out momentarily as the Helicopter flew directly over them and dipped its rotors as a wave. Mike watched, his heart sunk as he realised he had been missed, they had been looking at the bus, he turned to watch as once again another helicopter disappear and left him alone.

The next thing he heard was shouting, he looked to his left to see the 2 white pickups from the wedding party stopped on top of the Levee. The shouting started as about 5 or 6 men all looked and pointed towards him, a couple were no more than boys maybe 14 or15.

'Oh Fuck' Mike felt the elation and hope disappear and the dread take over, he knew he was too tired to run far, it was time to stand and fight. The posse began shouting to one another, AK47's began to appear, Mike looked around him, there was no real cover from fire, only from view, his only chance was to use the tall reeds to hide and try to Ambush them first. Mike made a run for the reeds, away from the men as they slid down the side of the bank, they were all armed, and unlike him had plenty of ammunition and were fresh, and all after him.

Once in the reeds Mike doubled back, he knew he had to move slowly, and carefully so as not to give himself away with too much noise, he also knew he had to be careful as any swaying of the reed tips could also give his movements away. He only moved for about 30 metres then stopped and laid down, he pulled out his Commando Dagger from its sheath, its long thin blade had been developed during the Second World War for silent killing Mike had never even opened an envelope with his, and it was only supposed to be there for the photographs, but now he held it tight in his right hand ready. He quietly loosened the strap holding his pistol so he could drop the knife and draw it quickly. He forced himself lower and he reaching behind and covered his body with some mud and a few bits of old reed. Like a Big Cat on the Savannah he silently waited, the only noise his shallow breathing and the pumping of his own heart.

If he was right they would spread out, 2 or 3 would probably come into the reeds and the rest would stay outside. About half the men looked old, so he hoped the young boys would be here in the reeds egged on by the older men to draw their first Infidel blood, they were young and inexperienced and should frighten easily, he needed an automatic rifle and maybe he could get one.

He could hear the voices of the men as they got nearer just as he had predicted he could hear the long reeds moving and the splash of water as someone moved through the reeds, he had to lay still, he could feel his heart beating, his breathing seemed so loud he imagined anyone could hear it, he could see the reeds moving to his left, then he saw him. It was one of the young boys, he spoke a few words and someone replied, another young voice but where was it coming from, he needed to see both or at least know where the other boy was, the young boy was very close, less than 10 metres away,

Mike was not happy about what he had to do, but it was them or me time, he wasn't sure if he could really do it, it looked easy in the movies, but this was real life and hoped he didn't have to kill either of them. Mike tried to lower himself further and tried not to look directly at the boy. If it went wrong now he was dead, the boy closed, and began to talk again, as he stopped talking Mike rose up, the boy turned too late, he grabbed his mouth but half missed, the top finger of his hand went into the boys mouth, the boy struggled and bit down, Mike drew the dagger up in front of the boys eye's then put the cold steel against his throat, the boy shocked and stiff with fear dropped his gun into the water at his feet, he and put both his hands on Mikes wrists gripping them hard. Mike was whispering in his ear, 'Shhh, shut up you fucker, Im not going to kill you, shh, shh', the boy stopped biting, he realised he should have been already dead and froze, this was just the result Mike wanted, he only wanted the gun. 'OK mate, you can run along now, *imshi OK, imshi,* but Shh, OK, Shh, OK' the boy seemed to understand and nodded, and mumbled 'Okay' through Mikes hand. Mike keeping the hand over his mouth sheaved the knife and drew his pistol, he turned him a little, and now put the pistol to the boys eyes, then took his hand off his mouth and moved around in front of him, Mike knelt down and picked up the rifle, when he had it in his hand he pointed to the Magazine, the boy understood and still frightened reached under his robe and produced another magazine, Mike indicated for more, but the boy shook his head. Mike holstered his pistol, and clicked off the safety of the AK, he then motioned for the boy to disappear as the boy turned away the reeds parted once again and another young boy stepped into view, this one was slightly older and the look of hate in his eyes he recognised from the night before, the first boy was in the way, and froze, there was a shout of alarm as he raised his rifle towards Mike, but Mike was a lot quicker, he pulled the trigger, nothing, shit its not even cocked, Mike dived to one side cocking the weapon as he did so, the boy opened up on automatic, as he did so the rifle recoiled and jolted uncontrollably in his young angry hands and the bullets sprayed everywhere. The younger boy leapt into the air with a scream as a single round found his heart and he dropped dead. Mike came up on aim and fired 2 shots into the chest of the older boy, he fell first onto his knees, the look of shock and pain obvious in his eyes, he knelt for a split second before falling face first onto the body of the other boy. Mike looked down at the ugly waste, the boys back was torn open where the two wounds had joined to make one large hole.

Mike moved forward, he didn't really want to do it but it was the only cover available so he got down on his knees behind the body's, he could hear the shouting and knew they were closing on him, he unclipped the magazine on his weapon and checked it, their was only one bullet left, shit, they had just been to a wedding so had probably let off most of his rounds into the air. He changed magazines, he hoped the others had forgotten to put on a fresh mag on as well but doubted it, these were older men, perhaps soldiers at one time, no doubt with experience fighting the Iranians here in their own border lands. He checked the older boys body and clothing, he a small leather bag on his belt, it had a magazine, and one on the other AK47, Mike left the magazine on, opting to leave it on the floor and use the other rifle as a spare in case he needed it.

The anger was really building up in Mike now, the death of the 2 boys had pissed him off, he blamed the older men, too lazy or afraid to come in themselves. Now he would have to kill them all, he now wanted to kill them all, and that was pissing him off as well. He waited, he could hear the reeds parting up ahead they were getting closer. Mike expected that they would not want to be separated and so at least be close enough to see each other, he probably had to kill the 2 or 3 in the centre almost immediately. If it went on too long two things could happen, either he would run out of Ammunition, or those on the outside of the line would come around and outflank him. Then with nowhere else to go and outnumbered it would be only a matter of time before they wore him down and got him. He knew he could not expect to be treated well, especially when they saw the 2 young bodies.

The first face appeared very close, Mike fired 2 shots in quick succession, both hit and the old man fell back through the reeds, almost immediately all hell broke loose, automatic fire came from every direction, it cut through the reeds above his head, pieces of grass flew everywhere. Mike flinched and forced his body as low as he could behind the bodies, the fire was fear-provoking but Mike soon realised they were firing blindly and just wasting ammunition. Now he had to watch both left and right, he would shoot one more time expecting the same indiscriminate barrage which he could use to crawl away as fast as possible to a new position.

He waited, the noise of reeds moving seemed to come from all around, but more slowly now, they were obviously moving more cautiously. Then he saw a glimpse to his right, the top of a cream head scarf, only a few metres away, Mike considered using his knife. If he could take this guy down silently then he'd be at a serious advantage, the others would pass him and not realise, but the rifle was too comfortable in his hands now, it was a proven weapon, and not easy to give up. Mike briefly checked around him, he could hear movement to the left but it was a little further away, he took aim in the general direction of where the scarf should now be, a reed moved and the head appeared clearly through the gap. 2 shots broke the silence, 2 solid thumps confirmed both good body shots, the old man swung through the reeds as he fell. Mike followed the body down with his Kalashnikov; the old man had been armed with a long bolt action rifle, mounted with a telescopic sight. As he fell the gun was pointing in Mikes direction, realising the old man was not dead Mike took aim, but automatic fire once more rained down around him, he threw himself back and crawled away as a louder and sharper single shot fired out and whistled

171

over his shoulder. Mike felt the rush of air and was temporarily deafened in his left ear as the snipers bullet just missed him.

The other man with the automatic weapon had been close, but was moving away fast. Mike couldn't let him go, he would run for help. There was also now a vehicle on the Levee that he could use. Mike rushed after the fleeing man, his weapon tucked under his arm pit as he used his left hand to push at the reeds. He was now close to the edge of the cover, and he saw the back of an old man running across the open ground. Mike raised his rifle, shit he couldn't shoot him in the back.

'STOP, STOP' Mike shouted hoping he would stop or at least turn to take a shot at him, and give him the excuse. He kept running, Mike took aim and fired 2 shots at him, water splashed up around his feet and the old man stumbled but kept going. Mike carefully aimed again, this time aiming high to offset the bad sights, at least one of the rounds found its target albeit a little low and the man fell, rolling on his back and gripping his thigh, screaming. Mike knelt for a moment, to take a breath, his lungs were burning with the effort.

Just then he heard a burst of gun fire, a hail of bullets hit the swamp just beside him. He looked up to see a man by the pickup, he had a light machine gun its twin bipod legs leaning on the tailgate. Mike stumbled and dived back into the cover of the reeds, the bullets were falling all around him.

He made it and the firing stopped, this guy was good, he wasn't wasting ammunition. There was only one thing to do, he made his way back down the inside edge of the reeds until he found the trail he had made. He followed it back to the old man, he was still alive and groaning, the sniper rifle was an old Russian Draganov, Mike snatched it from his hand, on his belt the old man had a spare magazine in a small pocket, Mike checked the magazine, it felt heavy, and he could at see at least four 7.62 calibre rounds, and hoped it was full which would give him ten round. Mike chambered a new round, and removed the old magazine; he put on the new one hopefully giving him eleven rounds. He slung the AK47 over his back, and made his way back to the edge of the reeds.

Slowly and carefully he crept forward, picking up an old piece of reed he held it over the black barrel of the gun, and eased the barrel forward in the direction of the pickup. He could see the figure stood on the roof, he was using a set of binoculars to search for Mike. Mike pulled the rifle butt into his shoulder and looked through the sight; he lined the cross hair over the figure on the roof. Mike immediately recognised the face and the chequered shirt.

Mike took his time; the figure was steady in his sight, the cross hair rested in the centre of his chest. He watched as he lowered his binoculars, gently pulling on the trigger he felt the first pressure then the sharp report as the butt powered back into his shoulder. Releasing the 7.62 round toward the target, Mike flinched for a second, but quickly recovered and looked through the sight. The man spun to the right, the binoculars thrown clear as he fell from the roof into the back of the pickup. Mike watched nothing moved, he saw a flash of black hair as the head appeared and disappeared. Mike pulled back the bolt, the empty cartridge ejecting to his right and re chambered a new round. He aimed at a section of rust on the side panels on the back of the pickup and fired again. This time he saw the hole appear; the sight was not zeroed to him and was well off to the right. He had missed the man on the roof, but only just.

Mike re cocked the gun, and took aim to the left of the rust patch, just as he squeezed the trigger the figure threw himself from the back of the truck, just escaping the bullet that easily pierced the aluminium side panel. Mike scanned the truck, trying to find his target, then he saw a flash and heard the Light Machine Gun, the bullets struck the reeds to his left. He had almost found his target; he could see the barrel just to the right of the back tyre. But the firer was hidden from him, Mikes had been a fool not to

173

change position, but was also afraid to lose sight of his quarry, the rifle he was using was also over oiled and was giving off a puff of smoke after each shot.

The tables had turned, Mike was now at a disadvantage, it was time to change the stakes. Mike only had 3 rounds left in this magazine, and 4 left in the original one. He took aim at the bottom of the truck; he could just see the bottom of the petrol tank. He took careful aim and fired, the round hit and he could see a stream of liquid pouring out, Mike quickly cocked the gun, and took aim again, this time aiming at the base of the chassis. To the left he saw a shadow, the figure was moving back, aware of the new danger. Mike squeezed, the round ricocheted off of the steel chassis and sparked, the flash enveloped under the chassis, a stream of flame poured from the tank, Mike was amazed it worked, but it was not the effect he had hoped for, and his enemy would have time to escape.

Mike felt the heat hit him in the face as the tank of petrol suddenly exploded probably a few seconds too late, it forced the back of the pick up into the air and ripped the aluminium back to pieces. The thick black smoke mushroomed up into the air. A figure appeared from the back running and screaming down the road, his white dish dash a ball of flames. Mike took aim, judging a small lead ahead of the figure, this time the single round hit its mark first time, spinning him to the ground and out of his burning misery.

The black smoke was billowing into the air, and would be seen for miles. Mike looked at the magazine in his webbing, it had 4 rounds left, he replaced the empty magazine on the rifle and waited. He was exhausted and couldn't run anymore, he needed to stand and fight.

It didn't take long, before they arrived 2 pickups appeared on the levee, Mike watched through his sight, both were full of men, one of which he thought was probably the RPG man from the night before. He stood up with the RPG by his side, looking out over the reeds. Mike needed to find out if anyone was in charge, so he aimed steadily at the figure and shot him straight through the heart, he fell forward and onto the floor. Mike watched as a man with a white cloth on his head began to shout at the others, as they dived for cover behind the vehicle, and the other side of the levee. Mike squeezed off a round at the fleeting leader but missed, another round wasted.

It wasn't long before they had regrouped and had obviously come up with a plan. He saw a couple of heads behind the levee moving to the left and behind the burning pick up. They knew that moving across the open ground was suicide against a sniper; they would outflank him and hunt him through the reeds. Mike had a decision to make he couldn't move out into the open just in case more Militia turned up on the Levee, he would be caught in the open. If he stayed where he was he would soon be overrun. Mike decided to take the risk and try for the vehicles up the outside of the reeds, a little risky but at least he could use the rifle, and then dash the last 150 metres across open ground. The ground was uneven and hard work, but the searchers should be blind to him due to the reeds.

Mike crawled on his knees for a little, then in a crouch he made a line into the open and towards the vehicles. If you were going to make a bold move it was always best to do it early on, it seemed to be working so far, and surprise was still on his side.

He was now only about 100 metres from the levee when a shot rang out from the reeds, he had been spotted. Mike dived down and pulled the rifle back up on aim, he searched carefully along the front of the reeds. Nothing, no movement and nothing caught his eye. Then another round burst from the cover, this time Mike saw the muzzle flash, he adjusted his aim, there was a shadow, but nothing definite. Mike waited, then he saw it, a figure moved behind the reeds, Mike fired, his target fell back, then once again all hell broke loose.

Smoke and flashes appeared all along the frontage, everywhere around him automatic fire sent water and marsh grass flying. Mike buried his head as low as he could and talked out loud to himself, 'bastards, now I'm fucked'

They were obviously a better drilled team than the last group. The guy at the edge must have seen him, and warned the others before he took his shot, now they would all be taking positions along the reeds. Mike crawled back a metre then moved to his right a little; he found a small hollow and carefully came back up on aim. He would only get one shot off before he would have to move again; Mike wasn't sure how many times he would get away with it.

Mike eased the rifle up and looked down the sight, he slowly scanned along the reeds, and couldn't see anything. Mike then looked across the top of the reeds at the bushy tips. 2 were swaying in the still air. He followed them both down and at the base of each he picked out a shadow. The closest one to the right was fidgeting, and gave quite a good target. Mike squeezed the trigger, as he pulled back he saw the tops of the reeds fall back as the body fell over.

The area was again peppered with incoming rounds, they must all be in position now and they obviously all knew where Mike was. Now they knew how close to the trucks he was, the danger was that one or two of them would go back out and around. If they made it to the vehicles they would be higher than him and he would be out flanked.

Mike decided to get in a position where he could watch the gap where the reeds stopped and the levee began, and where he could stay hidden from the main group. Mike crawled again to the right, and found a small gully that gave him a good view of the vehicles to his right, but more importantly the bank of the levee, and the edge of the reeds.

He settled in, the rifle laid in the direction of where he expected them to appear, and waited. It wasn't long before he saw the first head appear, the face shone as it looked in his direction, then for some reason fired a single shot.

Suddenly the area around him was bursting with fire again, they were trying to keep his head low and move their team into position. Luckily Mike had put himself in a position of advantage. He aimed, and waited, 2 figures began to climb the bank together, Mike hit the first one in the ass, and he fell back down the bank writhing in agony. Mike cocked the gun and took aim on the second, he was running out of time and fired, and missed. Mike cocked again his last round, the figure had made it to the top and dived over as Mike fired. The figure disappeared over the bank, Mike had to assume he had missed and was now in serious trouble, and about to be out flanked from an elevated position.

He pulled the AK47 off of his back and checked it over, making sure the selector was on single shot. The sight was a basic iron sight, and had already proved it would not be good enough to pick off the enemy at the edge of the reeds one by one. He had to now be prepared for the guy on the levee, it was only about 80 metres away. Mike put his back against the ditch he was in, so that he was still hidden from the reeds. His rifle in his shoulder he watched and waited, he hadn't noticed before but he was at another disadvantage, he was now looking almost directly into the sun. It was hard to see clearly but he knew he would be lit up to his enemy.

Mike saw the shadow appear from the corner of his eye, he swung the rifle around, but the guy was already looking down at him, the RPG aiming straight at him, Mike let off a round in the general direction and dived forward as he saw the burst of flame and smoke as the rocket launched.

It exploded 10 metres to his left, he felt as if his body had imploded, his hearing was muffled, and he felt dizzy and sick. Mike recovered a little; he heard rounds coming down around him again. Mike began to crawl, dragging himself forward, it wouldn't be enough. The grenade had missed that time but now he had his aim, he wouldn't miss again. Mike could hardly move, he was grabbing chunks of grass and pulling himself along the wet ground, trying to breath through the thick, chocking cordite, smoke and dust.

Mike had run out of options and had to do something, he wasn't going to just wait for the end. Using what little strength he had left he rolled over onto his back, and held the rifle in his shoulder again. He stared into the bright light again, then saw a shadow, he fired round after round in quick succession, then he heard the clunk, as the bolt clunked forward, but no round fired. He was out of ammunition. Mike felt around for a new magazine, fumbling, as his mind was no longer co-ordinating with his body, the shadow disappeared. Mike sensed something to his right, he looked around, a tall man in a chequered shirt was stood next to him, his familiar eyes ablaze. He was aiming his rifle straight at Mike's chest, and was shouting in a torrent of loud and furious Arabic.

Mikes heart sunk, and he dropped his rifle to his side, and stared up helplessly at the muzzle of the gun facing him. Mike looked into the grey eyes as the sound of the rifle fired and Mike just shut his eyes, his fight was over. He felt the pain as something hit his stomach hard, and his body involuntarily sat up in agony. But the pain stopped, Mike opened his eyes and saw the man laying across him, the AK47 between them on his stomach.

Mike hears more firing, as he tries to make sense of what is happening, a gun battle ensued around him, Mike used his last ounces of energy to wriggle out from under the body, pushing the dead weight off to one side. Just as he was free a figure appeared above him, the sun producing a dark silhouette of a large man, his weapon glinting off of the morning light, he wouldn't escape this time.

'Mike, thank fuck' Sven knelt down next to him, and grabbed his shoulders in a hug, 'OVER HERE, I've got him' Mike grabbed at Sven's webbing and with his head against his chest sobbed.

Chapter 11
Hortons' Light Foot

Mike looked around at the inside of the helo, the mood was jovial, the relief on everyone faces was obvious, every now and then someone would catch his eye, and smile, and put their thumbs up. Mike felt proud, and lucky, he loved these guys, he loved what he did, what he was a part of. His eyes welled up and turning his body to face the rear and with his hand on his forehead he cried.

After a few moments he began to think of getting home and seeing everyone else, probably in the pub. What would they think if they knew he was crying, they would take the piss? Mike began to laugh at himself, he wiped his tears with his thumb and fore finger, and laughed some more. It was great to laugh out loud when no one could hear you, and Mike laughed and laughed.

After only a few minutes in the air the Chinook was banking, below he could see the hastily built camp, he could clearly see a group of soldiers desperately holding onto the canvas of a half erected tent, and trying to cover their eyes as the down draught of the powerful helicopter blew sand and brush in a tornado.

Mike smiled to himself, especially as the chopper began to descend onto a road that was raised on top of a levee, it touched down. The aircrew man lowered the ramp a further half a metre and signalled to the guys, Mike ran off the back over the ramp, he was comforted to note that guarding the ends of the road either side of the chopper were Scimitar vehicles. Mike suddenly felt safe again, and no longer alone.

Gris led Mike and the lads 100 metres down the road to the camp entrance. As they jogged at Mikes weakened pace down the levee the camp was below them on the right, about half the size of a football pitch, it was surrounded on each side by barbed wire on top of a mound of sand. At each corner was a bunker, made of sandbags, all still under construction by half naked soldiers.

The gate was a single length of concertina wire that two black soldiers were guarding, the wire was being held open by the biggest of the two, Mike looked him in the eyes as he came through 'thanks mate'

The black lad smiled 'welcome back Sarge'

Mike smiled, 'cheers'

A familiar face was coming up to greet him, it was the young Lieutenant from Basra, 'Welcome back Sergeant Cole, good to see you out safe, how are you feeling'

Mike had some many emotions in the last few hours he wasn't quite sure how he felt, 'relived, and exhausted'

Just behind the Lieutenant was another officer, 'this is Major Curtis, the Company Commander'

'Well done Sergeant, you did a great job, sorry it took us so long'

'Thanks Sir, I was happy for the help, no need to build me a whole camp tho…eh!' Mike indicated to the bunker being constructed near by

Breakfast at Babs'

'Well there's no room left at the Basrah Hilton, so we have prepared a 5 star tent for you here, with a 1 star cot bed'

Thanks I'll think I'll go check in for a couple of hours'

'Well your lads insisted we have a bed ready for you, I will see you when you're ready for a debrief'

'OK Cheers'

Gris had been stood beside Mike, he pointed towards the nearest tent, 'were in here mate. This is your pit, and here's your 3rd line kit, the solar showers are straight out the other door'

'Eh Gris, thanks mate' Mike looked around the other lads were dropping their kit down, he could see they were all exhausted, all the adrenaline that had been pumping through their bodies over the last 2 or 3 days was leaving them as they relaxed, and came down.

'Thanks guys, what a bloodyin trip eh'

Mike sat on the end of the bed and stripped, he sat naked on the end of the bed and he opened his green bag. Third line kit was a spare rucksack or kit bag that you packed with non essential items and spare clothes that caught up with you when you needed them. That was the theory, and Mike was pleased to see it work when he really needed it, he pulled out a clean towel that smelt so fresh, his flip flops, shower gel and a toothbrush.

The shower area was just underneath the road, screened off by black hessian on wooden poles, wooden pallets made up the floor over shallow drainage ditches dug into the sand. Mike stepped in suspended on a gallows were 2 camping showers, transparent plastic bags which were heated by the sun. Mike unclipped the hose to release the water and was hit by the freezing water 'shit' Mike shivered. Gris had just stepped in beside him 'heating's off again then'

'Bloody hell mate, we were worried you'd gone down, we tried to look but they came from everywhere, and we had the kids, then we had to fight everyone to get back here'

'Hey Gris don't worry man, you did the right thing, you took charge and you did what you had to do, and if we weren't naked and covered in soap I'd give you a sloppy kiss'

'Well sod the soap' Gris leaned forward and threw his arm over Mike's shoulders, 'I'm glad we found you'

Mike returned the hug 'me too mate'

'Shitty death, can't you guys wait, we don't need to see any Gay love out here'

Marco let Mike go 'you're just jealous'

Sven jumped in, throwing his towel over the bar, 'anyone for. ….. manage a trios'

Mike walked back to the tent, the camp was busy, soldiers everywhere still putting up tents, stacking boxes of water, rations, digging trenches, preparing for a sustained operation. Mike sat on the edge of the cot and brushed off the dry sand that had collected on his damp feet. He laid back and fell into a deep and dreamless sleep. When he stirred the tent was full of chatter, the guys had pulled two cots into the middle of the tent and were sat playing cards on a wooden table crafted from a pallet.

Marco watched Mike sit up and rub his eyes.

'Ah its alive'

'Ready for a game of shithead'

'Maybe later, I need a pee' Mike was pulling on a fresh pair of combats and a t-shirt from his kit.

'Yeh, go out that door, Marco pointed to the open tent flap he had originally came in, go past the CP tent, and there's a gap in the fence, over the bank to the roses'

'OK cheers, is there water there?

'No you have to take your own, there's a box at the end of my pit, and there's alcohol gel by the shitters'.

Breakfast at Babs'

Mike looked at his watch, it was 5:15 he grabbed a 75 cl bottle of water from the box, and walked out of the tent. The light was greying, and Mike looked around there was the Command Post tent with its 8 metre mast holding the antennas for the radio's, held up by a mass of wires that needed avoiding especially at night. He walked toward the gap in the barbed wire that was marked by white tape, and continued over the bank to the other side. The white tape marked a route down the front of the bank for about 20 metres, about another 15 meters further on was the sandbag bunker now complete watching guard over the flat approaches on this side of the camp.

Mike found the row of 5 red plastic drain pipes sticking out of the ground, on the top of each was the rain catcher, a funnel to urinate into, the shape looking like a tall flower, a 'desert rose'. Mike looked out over the landscape; in the distance was a road, up on another levee, and what looked like the roof of a large building on the other side. The breeze was cool and fresh in his face, over to his left he saw the sun touching the horizon, he watched as the colours of the sky changed to a red, then purple, and by the time he had finished, the sun had disappeared. Mike was always amazed at how quickly the sun went down in the desert. He walked back towards his bottle, and washed his hands, it was now dark and Mike didn't have a torch. Carefully he wound his way back to the CP, and careful not to let any light in pushed his head in.

Sat at a wooden trestle table, like the ones decorators used for pasting paper for walls, was the signaller. Sat with his headphones on, signallers could always be found reading a fingered copy of FHM or Maxim Magazine, and always knew what was going on, in the world of the sexiest celebrities, latest must have gadgets and more importantly what was going on in Head Quarters.

'Hi mate'

The signaller looked around, 'Hi Sarge'

Mike cringed, 'where's the OC?'

'he's out Sarge, there's a patrol out tonight, and he won't be back till late tonight or early tomorrow'

'OK, no probs, thanks'

Mike wandered back to the tent, the cards were still fanned out on the makeshift table as the guys had a new game to occupy them, they were making lamps. Various methods were under trial and experiment. The best of which was an empty 2 litre water bottle, with the contents of a variety of coloured chemical sticks poured in. The most ineffective of which was a home made oil lamp from an empty pate tin from a ration box, a piece of rifle cleaning cloth and fuelled by liquid mosquito repellent.

'Shit Sven that stinks'

'Yeah, but it'll keep you from getting bitten'

'Yeah as long as we can stay in the tent with it!'

The games and banter went on into the night, the relief that they were all back together and the mission had been a success was obvious.

It was light outside when Marco shook Mike, hey mate, I just saw their OC, we fly out at 1310, and he asked if you'd go see him at least an hour before we go'

'OK cheers mate, what's the time now'

'Just gone 10, you looked like you were dead'

'Yeh I bloody needed that, now I need a shower and some scran'

'here mate you get your shower and I'll knock something up for both of us'

Mike had his shower and pulled on his uniform, out side the tent was a large square pit the lads had dug as cover against mortars, or fire. The edges were surrounded by sandbags that had been fashioned into seats. Marco was there with his large round aluminium pot, it was made from an old grenade tin. As Mike sat down he was passed a coffee by Sven, most of the lads were here cooking various concoctions, mostly noodle or pasta based.

Mike pointed at Marco's pot, 'you know they reckon the metal in them can cause cancer mate'

Well I got this pot when I threw my first grenade in training, and I've used it ever since, and I aint got anything yet…I don't think'

Sven took the offered coffee back off Mike 'That's because you only passed out at stand easy!' Stand Easy was a Naval term, a thirty minute coffee break each morning at ten O clock, he took a sip waiting for the comeback.

'I'll have you know, 15 years we've been together man and pot, I didn't pass out last bloody Tuesday like you.

Everyone laughed, there was a commotion up on the road, and everyone looked up to see a group of about 20 locals. Dressed in all standards and colours of Dish Dash, and running alongside them on either side were 4 British soldiers, shouting at the stragglers to keep up.

Mike pointed up 'What the hells going on up there, who's that motley crew?'

Marco started laughing, most of the guys were looking up watching the mess of bodies flailing up the road.

'That, that is Hortons' Light Foot!'

'No way. They don't look very light of foot to me, who are they?'

The CO, Horton, has decided to form a militia, from the local villages, they get $2 a day, and trained by the British Army!'

They'll have them doing soddin drill next; it'll be like Sharpe, all in a row, 2 rounds-a-minute lads!'

'Don't laugh but they have a parade square, up by the gate, for drill. They were there this morning clearing stones. Apparently the Great Colonial Emperor Horton is flying in today to inspect them himself'

'Yeah give them their $2 and pin medals on their chests!'

'That must be a lot of money for around here, let's hope we don't just leave them out to dry again eh?'

Mike was referring to the Marsh Arabs that had risen up against Saddam during the first Gulf War, at the request of the Allies and on a promise of freedom. The Allies that time of course stopped at the Iraq border and the Marsh Arabs paid for their revolution with their lives, slaughtered in huge numbers their bodies filled mass graves not far from the Allies furthest line of advance. Only now after more than 12 years the graves were being found.

'Oh we will leave them when we've had enough, just like the Kurds in the North, anyway get your laughing gear around that'

Mike took the pot, using a sand coloured scarf on the bottom to shield the heat, he tasted the meat balls and pasta, 'good mate, garlic's a little strong for brunch though'

Mike nodded, in the direction of the recruits, there was a lot of shouting going on up on the 'parade square' They were all watching now as the recruits were being taught how to march, with arms and legs swinging at the same time, in the Military this was called tick-tocking, it made Mike and the guys chuckle.

The Army are great eh, even out here they manage to make a Parade Square,

'I remember doing some training up in Catterick, there's an old estate there for urban training. When we'd finished we had a night of RnR before leaving the next day, There was a old bathroom with no wall, just open to the street, and someone had rigged up the old bath with a hose pipe and a paint pot with holes in' Mike took another spoonful of food 'So we all got naked, 60 or 70 blokes, all the officers, sergeants everyone and showered in 2 's and 3's, a right laugh, then we pulled our civvies out of our third line kit, all creased to buggery and headed out across the camp and ashore. I was with about 3 or 4 guys strolling across the car park when we heard this voice screaming' We looked around and there was this tall lanky RSM, marching with his stick, like you've never seen, must have been some sort of double double quick time, stick swinging, fuckin arms swinging, almost sprinting straight for us, well we began to bimble on, and we heard a shrill scream, HALT, HALT, you men HALT'

'We looked around, Shit me I think he means us, well we all stopped he was on us in about 20 seconds, 'You men' he screamed 'what do you think this is a holiday camp, bimbling like fucking fairies across my Parade Ground'

'One of the lads Bob answers him, 'Parade ground, sorry , eh Sir we thought it was the car park!'

Car park, fucking car park, do you see any fuckin cars'

'Bobs as matter of fact as you like,' 'No but its gone 3, I just though everyone had gone home'

'Well this just makes him worse, Right you lot, fall in, come on fall in, he's screaming at us again. We all looked at each other, still thinking he must be having a laugh, as he was about to scream another voice came from behind, 'something wrong RSM'

'The RSM looked around and there was the OC and Ops officer, also in creased Jeans and polo shirts, 'ah more volunteers for extra drill, good the more the merrier' he screamed, 'get over here', he then turned back to us, 'Not tonight RSM, but thank you for the kind offer, but unfortunately I have already given my officers and men permission to take a spot of RnR, you should have said earlier'

Marco was spooning more meatballs and noodles into his mouth 'Shitty death, what did he do?'

'well it was like something from Monty Python, he half turned, threw up a salute, and marched away, mumbling 'fucking Marines!'

After eating and swopping stories Mike went over to the CP tent he spent just over an hour with the Major conducting his debrief, he took Gris with

187

him to make sure that things tallied up and that he didn't miss anything
from the first phase before Mike was separated.

'Well Sergeant Cole, your men did a fantastic job, and Corporal Griswald
here would not let anyone relax for a minute, including me, my superiors
and my men.'

'I'm glad to hear it, and what of all the children?'

Well they are at the aid station at the moment, being fed ice cream last I
heard, I think they are being handed over to an local aid organisation, and
will go home to their families I suppose'

'OK great, poor bastards'

'Indeed could have been worse, if it wasn't for you guys' the Major
offered his hand 'I will send a signal to your unit when I return to camp, its
been a pleasure, maybe see you again soon'

'Not too soon I hope'

Mike shook hands with everyone in the tent and wished them all luck.

As they stepped outside the signaller ran out, 'Sarge, the choppers
inbound, you gotta go'

'Jesus it never stops, come on mate let's get the lads'

Mike and Gris rushed over to the tent, 'kit on guys, were off'

Sven was laying on his cot naked with just a flannel covering him up 'Oh
bugger…. my shits still everywhere'

Mike was in the same state, but still had to take charge, 'well we aint got
time to arse around, let's get it together, don't leave anything behind'

'Gris make sure everyone's got all their weapons and equipment'.

As the guys ran out to the gate, the Scimitars were already blocking off
the road, and once outside they shook out into formation, either side of
the road, and weapons in the shoulder, Mike looked back as the lads
naturally spread out, the guys at the back knelt down to open up the
spacing and were obviously alert watching their allocated arcs. Mike felt
proud, these were his men, and he was once again leading them, and

because of the way personnel were constantly moving around, on course, being promoted or drafted, this was probably the last time they would ever work together as a single unit again.

They made their way up the road until they were about half way between the 2 armoured vehicles; here Mike dropped his Bergan and went to ground on the bank. On seeing this everyone stopped where they were and found some cover.

Marco moved forward and joined Mike, 'hurry up and wait…nothing changes.

'No and it never will'

They waited had for about 15 minutes, Mike was just about to take them all back, it was not good practice to wait in one place for too long, and anyone watching would surmise that a helicopter was in bound, and maybe have time to set something up. The difference of course was that if these guys were going to stay, the enemy would have plenty of time and opportunity to take a shot or two.

Marco heard it first, 'I got it over to the west'

Then a shadow appeared hard to identify because of the sun, then it took shape a dark green Puma coming in very low from over the other side of the camp.

'Mike crouched up, OK guys close up,' he shouted over to Gris on the other side of the road, 'Gris stay that side with your stick'

The Puma had a door either side so the guys closed up in 2 lines or sticks, with the stick commanders, Mike and Gris at the front.

Anyone that still had ski goggles put them on, Mike regretted leaving his in his kit, the helicopter came over the top and flared up. A vortex of sand and dust was forced in ears and up noses, Mike smelt the welcoming smell of Avcat, but not the blast of hot air from the exhaust. As the helicopter squatted on its hydraulic suspension, Mike looked at the Aircrewman, he swung his gun out and held his hand up…..wait.

Some one was getting off first, a group of 3 or 4 , first out was a tall skinny man with wiry grey hair, he turned and collected his day sack from the aircrewman. As he turned again Mike could make out the Lt Colonel rank slide on his jacket. Must be the CO, he was followed closely by his Regimental Sergeant Major, a burly dark haired man.

Marco was just behind him and shouted in his ear, 'Emperor Horton!'

As they passed the Lt Colonel grabbed Mike by the hand, with his mouth close to Mike's ear he shouted above the thunderous noise of the Puma.

'Well done man, good to see you out safe'

Mike shouted 'thanks Sir, good to be dry again'

The Lt Colonel nodded and moved on, the RSM was carrying a bergan on his back, and as he passed he gripped Mikes shoulder with his large hand, squeezed it as he nodded a big friendly smile to Mike, and shouted 'Good effort' tapped once then left. Mike nodded in return.

He looked now back towards the aircraft, the Aircrewman was leaning out, holding onto the top of the door and gave Mike the thumbs up. Mike led the lads forward, then by the door he waiting letting the guys by, he patted each one on the shoulder as they passed, and watched them load. They had their heavy bergans slung on their left shoulder, with their weapons in their right hands. As they got to the door they had to throw the bergan up to the aircrewman who pulled them to a space in the centre where he piled them up. Mike watched him struggle with the guys kit, as Marco got on he began to give him a helping hand, the relief was obvious.

Col was last and smiled at Mike as he pulled himself into the chopper. Mike then swung his bergan on, which was light compared to the rest. The loadmaster put it on top of the pile; he then climbed on board and sat opposite the open door. The Aircrewman pointed at the large headphones hung above Mikes head. He then swung his machine gun back into position then looked down the line to check his passengers, he then looked at Mike and nodded, Mike gave him the thumbs up and they lifted off.

Mike put the headphones on and waited, the trick was to listen first as the Pilot and crew had a lot going on during take off and landing, so you waited. It wasn't always obvious who was talking to who, or even when they were talking to you. The soft microphones made all the voices sounded similar and they had their own slang. Mike had learned the best thing was to wait until the tone of voice changed to a questioning one, and no one else answered, normally some thing like, 'everyone cosy in the back' At the moment though, the chatter was serious.

'all secure…..roger….clear left…..clear right…..tail clear……wheels light……OK coming around large sweep to Port………vehicle and people in the field south…..Roger seen……'

The chopper flew around in a long arc, then back over the camp,

'……look at that lot down their…..its Lawrence of Basrah…..'

Mike tapped Sven on the shoulder and pointed toward the Parade Square.

There below were the Light Foot, fallen in and marching down the line was the Colonel, a long thick red feather protruding from his beret. As the Puma flew over the feather began to quiver, a hand lifted on top of his beret but the inspecting officer never faltered.

'….OK….how are the Marines today?'

Mike thumbed the small press to talk switch 'yep good thanks, where are you taking us?'

'that's what I was going to ask you, we are on an admin run, between Basrah and Al-Amarah…..the Colonel we just dropped off said to take you where ever you wanted to go'

'great, you got enough fuel for Bangkok?'

'not quite, how about Basrah logs base'

'that was going to be my second choice, Paris of the South!'

Mike nudges Col and shouted in his ear, 'Basrah' Col nodded and passed the message down. He looked around the cabin and watched everyone's faces, they were all smiling, or laughing the tension of the last few days was beginning to release its grip. They were still in hostile territory, still had to get organised, and still had to get home, but at least they were heading in the right direction.

Chapter 12
Dutch Courage

It had been a long day of debriefing and sorting out kit, but Mike had told all the lads to stop whatever they were doing and be in the bar by 1930.

When Mike walked in it was already busy, and the lads had commandeered a large round table in the corner.

Sven was leaning back in his chair a can of beer in his hand 'Hey Mike you just been on the BBC news'

'Right that's all I need'

'It was just an after piece, mainly about the elections, then said a combined rescue mission was launched after a Marine was separated from his team, and that was it, your 15 minutes of fame in 10 seconds!'

'Yeah and that's 10 seconds too bloody much'

Mike went to the bar to order a drink, the bar maid came over.

'Got your beer chit'

Mike pushed the small blue card on to the bar and the girl was about to stamp today's date box. She always seemed to be in a mood, so the lads had nick named her 'Helga'

'Are you the Marines that rescued those kids?'

'Yeah how did you know about that?'

'A couple of the girls work in the HQ, and they listened in to the whole thing'

'OK, you girls got this place stitched up haven't you?'

'Of course, were girls!'

The girl stamped the card, but to Mikes surprise she stamped a box, and not one of todays.

'Cheers love, what's that for?'

'Well you probably need a drink after all that babysitting'

Mike walked back over to the lads and sat down, he was about to tell them about the bar maid when a familiar face came up to the table. Dressed in Desert combats but with a cross on his insignia and placed 8 beers on the table, Mike acknowledged the guy 'thanks, what are they for?

'God bless you lads, for Pat, good job, great job' the figure walked away and out the bar, Mike was still staring as Marco came over, 'hey wasn't that the Padre from the Galley Tent, what did he want'?

'Is that Patrick Milton free?'

'Yeah the SAS and SBS went in and got him out a couple of days ago whilst you were on the run, that's another reason for the delay getting you out'

'Bloody Sky Pilots are great eh!' Sky Pilot was one of many terms used for the clergy who served.

'What do you mean, Mike?'

'He obviously saw us all tooled up before we left, swaggering around like we owned the place, all the black kit, he thinks we did it!, he thinks we got that hostage out! Well no point running after him now, I'm sure the boys won't mind us drinking their beers, cheers'

Gris came across with a huge grin on his face,

'OK guys Uncle Jimbo's been busy and we've hit the jack pot, those Naafi girls behind the bar that we have been flashing our teeth at have heard all about our hero' Gris pointed with first fingers of both hands at Mike, 'and they want to hear the whole story, they want a private audience with the *Hero of the Lake'*, Gris used those 2 fingers again sweeping them around pointing at the lads, 'and his band of brothers, 'and you'll never guess where?' he paused for effect as everyone waited 'only in their own private bar, and guess where it is?'

Sven leaned back in his chair, 'I know, Saddams Yacht?'

'And our survey says….uh uh, no better than that'

'A hands-free bar on Pataya beach?

'Close, but I don't think you'll get a blow job, its in the bloody beer store!'

Mike pushed back the plastic chair and immediately stood up 'OK, what we waiting for, let's go'

'ah now, don't be too hasty, we've got to wait for the 2 delectable ladies to call last orders then we go, I've even got us a driver and green limousine organised, and you'll never guess who the driver is, remember the Irish Nurse from the Herc?'

Well she only treated the little girl for her scratches and after hearing a slightly embellished story by yours truly, she also wants to toast the *Hero of the Lake*! And she gets off duty at closing time, but don't thank me now, you can all buy me a drink later'.

As usual the bar was shut exactly on time and an army Staff Sergeant came strolling in to ensure everyone left and the place was locked up. The guys walked out of the pub, and over to a single porta-cabin that housed a small 'Subway' and a 'Peppe's pizza'

Marco was stood on the steel steps at the bottom of Peppe's 'Gris we got time for some scran before the Limo arrives'

Just as Gris was about to answer when a soft Irish voice called over, 'only if I get a slice'

Marco looked over there was the nurse leaning on a long wheel based Land Rover, her blonde hair was in pig tails,

Sven was just audible, 'fuck me….please!'

Marco waved the menu at her, 'not sure about a slice, but I'll give you a portion!'

Everyone cringed not sure whether to laugh at Marco's quick double-entendres, but you never risked upsetting the driver until you had arrived at the destination, so there was only a little sniggering.

But the Irish whit was quick in reply, 'No I only want a slice from you, and no Sausage!' and everyone breathed a sigh of relief, and laughed at Marco instead.

'Fair one, is spicy chicken OK'

Everyone piled into the back of the Land Rover, designed for 4 there were now 7 in the back, Ginge, and Marco were on the floor in the centre, everyone else was crammed on two PVC bench seats with their backs against the canvas.

Mike and Gris were the lucky ones crammed into the front, the Nurse who Mike had discovered was called Jill was driving the unyielding 4 x 4 with gusto. Mike watched in admiration how she managed to kick down the heavy clutch and turn the wheel on beast, yet still keep her shy, girl like demure.

They were following a short wheel based Land Rover with the canvas removed, the 2 girls from the bar were being driven by the third member of the bar team a young lad who looked like he should still be at school, so the lads had nicknamed him Skin.

Breakfast at Babs'

The Land Rovers pulled up, and Liz the chief barmaid, the lads called 'Helga the Bar Commandant', walked up and unlocked the door, she looked at Mike and gesturing the opening door, said, welcome to 'The Glory Hole'

'Thanks Liz' Mike stepped into a cold dark room, his eyes were trying to make sense of a few silhouettes when something hard hit his chest, he was pushed back and fell to the ground, Mike reached forward, and as his hands felt hair, he was licked in the face by a large Dog.

The lights went on and everyone laughed as Mikes pinned to the floor by heavy paws, had his face washed by a golden retriever.

Mike looked around, it really was the beer store, but they had built a dividing wall with plywood, and made a small room. It had had plenty of soft seats and 2 big settees, surrounding a homemade coffee table. All along one end was a makeshift bar; it even had mirrors, and some optics.

'Where did you get the whiskey and vodka?'

'Ahh well all the civvies security companies get unlimited bars, so we do deals with them, want one?'

Mike knew it was going to be a long night.

Mike spent the last day with a thick hangover saying his good byes and thanking all the staff that had helped him prepare for the job. He spent most of the time recounting his story, which was a good rehearsal for when he got home.

He visited the RAF to organise the paperwork for the lads and the cargo, the guys were busy trying to repack all the equipment that had turned up that morning on the back of 2 trucks.

This time it went smoothly, at this end they didn't seem to care what they were carrying. On mentioning the problems he had had leaving the UK Mike then found out the rules were different because they were flying on a Galaxy.

Mike smiled to himself, he had never flown on one of these giant aircraft before, they were being rented from the Americans which may have been the reason for the simpler documentation process. The only thing that took a little time was converting all the weights on the kit from Kilograms to Pounds.

It was 0300 in the morning and the heat was like a summer's day at home, only dry. Of course that wasn't always so, it was often freezing in the desert at night. Basrah international airport was only a shell of its former self, a dusty ex international airport, all the little shops that resembled oversized gilded parrot cages that once would have sold the usual wares for departing visitors, above the walkways the usual signs in Arabic and some also in English.

All the guys were sitting now on the cold marble floor, leaning against the wall or resting their heads on bergans and day sacks. Everyone was quite obviously feeling the effects of the last few beers they had drunk earlier. Gris had unpacked and erected his folding cot bed and was already snoring, he got a kick from Sven and rolled over quietly.

Mike looked along the long corridor that would have once been bustling with businessmen and the wealthier Iraqi's that could afford or were indeed allowed to travel by air.

At the end was the arrival hall, which was now just a wooden desk, a short stocky RAF Sergeant was shouting at a large group of new arrivals. Mike watched they looked like Rabbits caught in the headlights of a truck, most were dressed in brand new desert camouflage and body armour, many of them wearing floppy hats that were still stiff and rigid from the stores always a good sign of newbies. Many probably straight out of training depots, a few were probably reservists; quite a number were young girls with bad fitting and unflattering combats, hanging off of them. They looked even more like they would stand dazed until the car ran them over.

'More meat for the mincer' Mike said quietly

Breakfast at Babs'

Gris was also sat quietly watching and contemplating the scene, 'I bet there were a few mothers tears when that lot had their apron strings cut from them'

'Was that us once?'

'Maybe at the train platform at Lympstone' Lympstone was the Commando training school where they had all done their training. It had its own platform called 'Commando Halt', where all new recruits arrived in the same condition, hair too long and in a state of shock.

'I remember my first drop into a field in South Armagh, I still remember the green glow of the instruments in the Lynx, and the feeling of apprehension, laying on the wet grass under the down draught of the helo, the smell of the aviation fuel, then it lifting off the incredible noise which faded in the distance, then the silence and that feeling of being all alone, but then you get up off the wet ground, at first shitting yourself, and you get on with it, but I'll never forget the feelings and the smell, and the apprehension. I don't expect this lot will ever forget this terminal building and the dusty smell and the dry heat in their throats'

They continued to watch the influx of uniforms with various shoulder flashes and ranks, they were all stood under the sign that said luggage collection point, the carousel began to turn and everyone realised that the whole planeload had identical issued black grips, so began the lucky dip. A young girl her blonde pony tail hanging out from under her desert hat had grabbed a trolley that squeaked as it rolled

Gris nudged Mike, 'she'd get it, the blonde'

'Seen' Mike was watching her trying to make out the shape of her arse under the baggy combats, everyone looked in her direction, the blonde sensed the stares and looked around, 6 pairs of eyes smiled at her, she blushed and turned back to trying to manoeuvre the trolley.

Everyone watched as she loaded the trolley with all her kit, all the lads knew that it was a fruitless task as just outside the Terminal Building was a line of concrete defences that you couldn't get a trolley through anyway, but this was just the type of small minded simple entertainment that was priceless. Just as she had built the pile high enough to make it unstable, the carousel stopped and the lights went out, everything was plunged into darkness.

A voice called from the gloom 'Its OK ladies and Gents', a large torch beam pierced the dark hall 'this happens a few times every night, it'll be about 15 minutes before they sort it out'.

Torches came out of bags and smaller streams of light broke through the dusty darkness, after only a few minutes there was a noisy jolt and the conveyor lurched into life, the lights flicker on and a loud cheer went up.

An RAF corporal was walking over to the group, 'is Sergeant Cole here' Mick stood up, 'what's up mate don't tell me, were 2½ days early and there's been a delay'

'No Sarge' Mike cringed once again, but let it pass, he continued, 'the Galaxy's on the pad ready for you, you're the only passengers so well process you now and get you straight on board'

'no way, well done mate you be careful with all that initiative, it'll get you in trouble around here, come on lads let's get the fuck out of Dodge'

For most of the lads including Mike it was the first time in a Galaxy, the guys walked out with their helmets, body armour and most carried a daysack with walkmans, sleeping bags and a few bits and pieces to make the flight a little more comfortable. It was only as they approached the plane that its enormity became apparent, the huge wings seemed to dip with the weight of the 4 jet engines, they climbed the access ladder and stepped into what looked like an aircraft hangar, up to the left were steps, at the top of which Mike could see a little of the cockpit. The cargo hold was massive uncluttered and well lit, quite the opposite to the Hercules.

They were shown to a bank of seats that were against the wall of the aircraft. They were blue, and cushioned and looked amazingly comfortable.

The load master, even had his own little open plan office at the front of the plane with a computer and swivel chair. Mike looked at the load, near the rear ramp was what was left of their boats the couple that didn't get used on the operation, all folded now on pallets, it seemed sad to have so little to take back, but at least they didn't leave anyone behind.

In the middle of the hold were a couple of stripped down Land Rovers, they looked like Matchbox toys in there, Mike had heard that they used these aircraft to carry the Chinooks over.

It wasn't long before the load master came around to give them a brief, he gave them all a cardboard box with some snacks in, and offered everyone some foam earplugs, but everyone was seasoned enough travellers to have brought their big shooting ear defenders as you could fit your walkman earphones on underneath.

This was Basrah airport and as the guys well knew from the last experience flying in, not the place to be hanging around, especially in such a huge and prestige target for the local insurgents, who could buy an RPG for about $50 at the local market, and at $10 a rocket it could well be open season.

'Yep, you flown one of these before?

'No never, you?'

Marco shook his head, 'I don't suppose they can be as noisy as a Herc, it like St Pauls in here'

As Mike began to speak the engines were started, one by one, and Mike was gradually drowned out, giving up he shrugged his shoulders and put his ear defenders on.

The lights in the cabin turned red and the huge bird gradually moved forward. Take off was not the usual lurch into the air, but felt smooth and graceful, the climb was steep, and as she levelled out everyone began to get comfortable.

Mike laid out his jacket on the floor and with his MP3 ear phones under his ear-defenders, drifted to sleep with Pink Floyd.

The sound of alarm bells rang and Mike was woken and sat up quick. He looked around in a half-daze, everyone was sleeping the load master was at his desk with a coffee playing solitaire. Then the bells again, as the intro to Money played, shit he kept meaning to delete that track from his player.

Awake now and a little hungry, he sat up and looked around, as usual there were bodies everywhere. Someone was using the cover over the back of one of the Land Rovers as a hammock, Marco was next to him dribbling into his jacket which was rolled up as a pillow, he'll be happy later when he had to put it on, Mike smiled.

Sitting up against the side he opened his box, obviously the American rental agreement didn't include a catering arrangement.

Loosely wrapped in Clingfilm was a sandwich with a thick lump of hard butter, and a slither of spam, so thin it looked like it had been run over by a steam roller, the edges that protruded were slightly darker where it had not been wrapped carefully enough and had dried. There was also a blue ribbon chocolate bar, a packet of almost out of date cheap crisps, almost always salt and vinegar, and a green apple, which was as hard as a boiled sweet and tasted like a cooking apple. Finally at the bottom the prize a small carton of '2 sips' orange juice, so called because you only got 2 sips. Primary school children had more nourishment in their lunch boxes, someone needed to call in Jamie Oliver.

Mike wondered whether to save the sandwich and orange for later on in the 6 hour flight. He couldn't resist and regretting his lack of will power as he scoffed the curled sandwich, and pierced the straw through the silver foil and had his 2 long draws emptying the carton.

Chapter 13
Breakfast at Babs'

Brize Norton was not the hive of activity it had been on the way out,
there were a few guys and girls in the green and brown of temperate
patterned uniform in the departures lounge as they walked through,
probably off to Europe, a few were travelling with their families. The guys
walked through, the look and feeling of elation must have been obvious to
the onlookers. Mike saw a little girl about the same age as the little girl in
the sheep shed, sat with her Dad. Mike caught her eye and he smiled a big
happy smile at her, the smile was returned, and then the girl went all shy.
Mike felt uplifted by the encounter, and bounded through and onto the
hire car desk.

The keys the girl gave him opened a new white LDV van, everyone
groaned; Mike opened the side passenger door first, well in this banger we
should be there by Christmas, just'

'Yeah this Christmas or next' Gris went around to the passenger side and
opened the side door for the rest of the guys, 'in you get guys, how nice of

the transport lads to break the budget and sort us out with something off of Pimp my Ride, or is it Scrap Heap Challenge'.

The kit was all loaded into a second transit van; Ginge was closing the back doors as Sven started the engine. Leaning out of the window he shouted over to Mike, 'hey Mike…..MIKE'

'Yes mate?' Mike saw the big cheesy grin on Svens face, something was about to happen

'last one back gets the beers in' the van revved and pulled away, Mike saw Ginge who was only half in, with the passenger door still open, fly back into his seat, and the door slammed itself shut as the van flew out of the car park.

'Right everyone in, come on lets go, we gotta catch him'

The race was on

Their only chance of catching the silver transit was on the downhill stretches, everyone on board was egging the bus to go faster, the speed gradually picked up, and now in the outside lane Mike was gaining.

The transit brake lights came on, now Mike knew he had Sven, his foot was flat on the floor and the dial was gradually creeping up twitching over 90, the transit van in front slowed drastically, someone shouted from the passenger seat, 'speed camera' it was too late as the double flash took their picture.

'bollocks' Mike looked in the rear view mirror, Sven was flashing his lights at him from behind, he was laughing so hard Mike imagined he could hear it. There was only one thing to do in a situation like this, Mike began to laugh shouting 'bastards' at the top of his voice, no one cared they just wanted to get home; and they were ahead, for the moment.

Mike was sat in the passenger seat as they pulled up first outside the gates of the Unit. Gris had driven the last hour since they had called a 20 minute truce and stopped on the M5 for a Burger King. They had won easily, but not because of the speed of the minibus.

Col had seen a Security guard in the service station car park and told him that he had seen a lot of strange looking gear and suspicious activity around the back of the silver transit. They watched as the security guard then approached two policemen in a patrol car. He pointed at Sven and Jim as they were running for the transit arms full of Burger King bags, obviously trying to beat the others to the exit. Everyone was looking back laughing as they saw the blue lights flashing and the patrol car pull forward to block the silver van trying to escape the scene.

Sven had since been on the mobile, it had taken a little while to explain who they were, both had changed into civvies and ID cards were buried in their kit in the back of the van.

Gris stopped by the locked gates and the MOD Policeman approached the van.

'Hey guys, I heard you were home, good to see you all back safe'

'Hi Frank, you miss us?'

'Yeah its been real quite around here, the rest of the lads have been on exercise up in North Devon, but their all back now, the message was armoury is open, leave your gear and get down the Pub'

'OK, don't bother shutting the gate we'll be back out in 20 mins, and the other wagons about 10 minutes behind'.

Mike was stepping out the shower as Sven ran in, 'bastards, those coppers saw a couple of pistol magazines and almost had us emptying the whole van, luckily Ginge found his gopping ID card'

The lads in the showers were still shouting abuse at Ginge as Mike walked out in his flip flops to the locker room.

The Pub was only 200 meters from the gate, it overlooked the camp and was one of 3 in the small village, but this one was theirs, the walls were adorned with memorabilia and photographs, and the landlord always made them welcome, he also managed to employ a few charming barmaids.

The squadron Christmas piss up was well under way and as the lads walked into the lounge, cheers went up, hands were shaken and pints of beer thrust into their hands.

Most of the lads were dressed up, fairies, Father Christmas, angels, Mother Christmas, and even 3 guys in old brown kit bags spray painted as cans of Fosters, Guinness and Bud, with only arms and faces showing, Mike laughed as he watched them struggle to reach their mouths with their beer glasses.

The atmosphere was jubilant, it felt good to be amongst the guys again, the CO came over, Mike smiled at the green tights and plastic flute he had tucked in his belt, Peter Pan grabbed Mikes hand, 'welcome home, and Merry Christmas'

'Cheers Sir, its good to be home, so where's Wendy?'

'Couldn't make it; she had to fly!'

Mike shook his head

'I hear you had quite an exciting time, you'll have to tell me about it tomorrow, when I'm not dressed like a tit, another beer?'

Mike laughed 'Aye Sir, Guinness, cheers'

No one had wanted to get up the next morning; they had a late start which was always welcome. Mike had woken up with the brides maid in his bed, he had to wake her up and send her away in a Taxi, he couldn't even remember where he'd caught up with her, or even if they had done anything last night, he'd remember eventually, not everything, but hopefully the good bits.

He walked into the tea boat to find it empty, a large yellow Post-It Note was stuck on the door, it simply said ' 10:00, Breakfast at Babs', Mike smiled and walked down the corridor. The canteen was full of guys, the lads were all sat at the same table that they had been at when he told them of the operation only 2 and a half weeks ago, Gris pushed a chair out for him, 'sit down mate, its all ordered 8 full breakfasts, and its on your tab' everyone laughed, Mike took the seat between Gris and Marco, 'I don't remember much, I woke up with that bird again' everyone laughed, 'don't you remember' the way Marco asked it was obvious there was going to be a story to follow,

'no I don't remember fuck all, what happened?'

As Jon told the story images began to appear in Mikes minds eye, but the puzzle never came together, 'well that blonde bird from behind the bar and your bird started kissing each other, with a bit of coaxing from all of us, then they had hands up each other's tops, and they were really getting into it'

'Yeah I remember now, its coming back' but then, 'oh Fuck I threw up'

Everyone laughed, 'yep and that was the end of that little fantasy, and your chances of a threesome'

'We'll probably a good job cause I wouldn't have remembered anyway'

'Alright you lot' it was Carole, her rich Devon accent calling over the counter, 'this should shut you up'

Everyone sat in silence working through the mountain of bacon, sausage, beans, mushrooms, black pudding and toast.

When he had finally mopped up his plate with the last piece of bread and butter Mike leaned back and looked around at the guys, his team all together as such probably for the last time, things changed so quickly half of the lads would be in new jobs before Easter 'well we did it, we said we'd laugh about it when we were all here, and here we are'.

Mike paused and looked around at the faces, somehow everyone looked different, there was now a depth behind the faces, a story and a maturity that wasn't there at the Wedding only a few weeks before, Mike spoke across the table to everyone, and no one, 'its always the same though, same shit, different fight, life still goes on with or without us'.

'Whatever we do, were still just pawns, and you know nothing's really changed in Iraq, and there's only one thing changed here since we've been gone; fuckin petrol's gone up another 5 pence'.

THE END

1489587R0

Printed in Great Britain by
Amazon.co.uk, Ltd.,
Marston Gate.